FORGIVE ME, LEONARD PEACOCK

By Matthew Quick:

THE SILVER LININGS PLAYBOOK
SORTA LIKE A ROCKSTAR
BOY 21
FORGIVE ME, LEONARD PEACOCK

MATTHEW QUICK

FORGIVE ME, LEONARD PEACOCK

headline

First published in Great Britain in 2013 by
HEADLINE PUBLISHING GROUP

1

Cataloguing in Publication Data is available from the British Library

Hardback ISBN 978 1 4722 0915 3
Trade paperback ISBN 978 1 4722 0818 7

Printed and bound in Great Britain by Clays Ltd, St Ives plc

Headline's policy is to use papers that are natural, renewable and recyclable
products and made from wood grown in sustainable forests. The logging and
manufacturing processes are expected to conform to the environmental
regulations of the country of origin.

HEADLINE PUBLISHING GROUP
An Hachette UK Company
338 Euston Road
London NW1 3BH

www.headline.co.uk
www.hachette.co.uk

For the lighthouse keepers—past, present, and future

I prithee take thy fingers from my throat,
For, though I am not splenitive and rash,
Yet have I in me something dangerous,
Which let thy wisdom fear. Hold off thy hand.

—From *Hamlet* by Shakespeare

ONE

The P-38 WWII Nazi handgun looks comical lying on the breakfast table next to a bowl of oatmeal. It's like some weird steampunk utensil anachronism. But if you look very closely just above the handle you can see the tiny stamped swastika and the eagle perched on top, which is real as hell.

I take a photo of my place setting with my iPhone, thinking it could be both evidence and modern art.

Then I laugh my ass off looking at it on the miniscreen, because modern art is such bullshit.

I mean, a bowl of oatmeal and a P-38 set next to it like a spoon—that arrangement photographed can be modern art, right?

Bullshit.

But funny too.

I've seen worse on display at real art museums, like an all-white canvas with a single red pinstripe through it.

I once told Herr[1] Silverman about that red-line painting, saying I could easily do it myself, and he said in this super-confident voice, "But you didn't."

I have to admit it was a cool, artsy retort because it was true.

Shut me the hell up.

So here I am making modern art before I die.

Maybe they'll hang my iPhone in the Philadelphia Museum of Art with the oatmeal Nazi gun pic displayed.

They can call it *Breakfast of a Teenage Killer* or something ridiculous and shocking like that.

The art and news worlds will love it, I bet.

They'll make my modern artwork instantly famous.

Especially after I actually kill Asher Beal and off myself.[2]

Art value always goes up once the artist's associated with fucked-up things such as cutting off his own ear like Van Gogh,

---

1 Herr Silverman is my Holocaust Class teacher, but he is primarily the German teacher at my high school, which is why we call him Herr and not Mr.

2 On Livestrong.com I read that "every 100 minutes another teenager will commit suicide." And I don't believe it's true at all, because why don't you ever hear about all of these suicides on the news or whatever? Do they all happen in secret or in other countries? Suicide can't be that common, can it? And if it is...here I am thinking I'm being daring and original with my own plans. Ha! Here's more damning evidence, regarding my uniqueness. According to Wikipedia—admittedly not the most reliable and in this case it's totally outdated—"In the United States, firearms remain the most common method of suicide, accounting for 53.7 percent of all suicides committed during 2003." Wikipedia also says, "Over one million people die by suicide every year." So according to Wikipedia, suicide takes care of one million fucked-up people every time our planet circles the sun. I wonder what Charles Darwin would have to say about that fun little fact. Natural selection? Nature's way of protecting the stronger and more necessary? Is my mind simply an agent of nature? Am I about to make Uncle Charlie Darwin proud?

or marrying his teenage cousin like Poe, or having his minions murder a celebrity like Manson, or shooting his postsuicide ashes out of a huge cannon like Hunter S. Thompson, or being dressed up as a little girl by his mother like Hemingway, or wearing a dress made of raw meat like Lady Gaga, or having unspeakable things done to him so he kills a classmate and puts a bullet in his own head like I will do later today.

My murder-suicide will make *Breakfast of a Teenage Killer*[3] a priceless masterpiece because people want artists to be unlike them in every way. If you are boring, nice, and normal—like I used to be—you will definitely fail your high school art class and be a subpar artist for life.

Worthless to the masses.

Forgotten.

Everyone knows that.

Everyone.

So the key is doing something that sets you apart forever in the minds of regular people.

Something that matters.

---

3 *Breakfast of a Teenage Killer* is a sick double entendre, as I am a killer who *is* a teenager, *and*—since my target is a teenager whom I must kill—I am also a killer *of* teenagers!

TWO

I wrap up the birthday presents in this pink wrapping paper I find in the hall closet.

I wasn't planning on wrapping the presents, but I feel like maybe I should attempt to make the day feel more official, more festive.

I'm not afraid of people thinking I'm gay, because I really don't care what anyone thinks at this point, and so I don't mind the pink paper, although I would have preferred a different color. Maybe black would have been more appropriate given what's about to transpire.

It makes me feel really little-kid-on-Christmas-morning good to wrap up the gifts.

Feels *right* somehow.

I make sure the safety is on and then put the loaded P-38 in an old cedar cigar box I kept to remember my dad, because he used to enjoy smoking illegal Cuban cigars. I stuff a bunch of old socks in to keep my "heater" from clanking around inside and maybe blasting a bullet into my ass. Then I wrap the box in pink paper too, so that no one will suspect I have a gun in school.

Even if—for whatever reason—my principal starts randomly searching backpacks today, I can say it's a present for a friend.

The pink wrapping paper will throw them off, camouflage the danger, and only a real asshole would make me open up someone else's perfectly wrapped gift.

No one has ever searched my backpack at school, but I don't want to take any chances.

Maybe the P-38 will be a present for me when I unwrap it and shoot Asher Beal.

That'll probably be the only present I receive today.

In addition to the P-38, there are four gifts, one for each of my friends.

I want to say good-bye to them properly.

I want to give them each something to remember me by. To let them know I really cared about them and I'm sorry I couldn't be more than I was—that I couldn't stick around—and that what's going to happen today isn't their fault.

I don't want them to stress over what I'm about to do or feel depressed afterward.

THREE

My Holocaust class teacher, Herr Silverman, never rolls up his sleeves like the other male teachers at my high school, who all arrive each morning with their freshly ironed shirts rolled to the elbow. Nor does Herr Silverman ever wear the faculty polo shirt on Fridays. Even in the warmer months he keeps his arms covered, and I've been wondering why for a long time now.

I think about it constantly.

It's maybe the greatest mystery of my life.

Perhaps he has really hairy arms, I've often thought. Or prison tattoos. Or a birthmark. Or he was obscenely burned in a fire. Or maybe someone spilled acid on him during a high school science experiment. Or he was once a heroin addict and his wrists are therefore scarred with a gazillion needle-track marks. Maybe he has a blood-circulation disorder that keeps him perpetually cold.

But I suspect the truth is more serious than that—like

maybe he tried to kill himself once and there are razor-blade scars.

Maybe.

It's hard for me to believe that Herr Silverman once attempted suicide, because he's so together now; he's really the most admirable adult I know.

Sometimes I actually hope that he did once feel empty and hopeless and helpless enough to slash his wrists to the bone, because if he felt that horrible and survived to be such a fantastic grown-up, then maybe there's hope for me.[4]

Whenever I have some free time I wonder about what Herr Silverman might be hiding, and I try to unlock his mystery in my mind, creating all sorts of suicide-inducing scenarios, inventing his past.

---

4 I Googled "How long does it take to die when you slit your wrists?" There are all sorts of people asking this question on the Internet and most of them say they are researching the topic for their high school health class. Most of the posted answers accuse the asker of lying and urge him (her?) to seek professional help. There are straight-up answers from people who claim to be doctors and others who have actually slit their wrists with razor blades and survived. They all say this is a very painful way to die (or not die)—that it's not peaceful, not at all the death-in-a-warm-bath-go-to-sleep type of deal in which movies make you believe. The blood can clot, which keeps you alive and in excruciating pain. But then I found posts about how to slit your wrists the "right way," so you will actually die, and that depressed me, because people actually post stuff like that, and, even though I wanted to know the answer, so I could weigh my options, that info maybe shouldn't be on the Internet. I'm not going to list the right way to slit your wrists or explain it to you, because I don't want any additional blood on my hands. But really—why *do* some people post the correct ways to commit suicide on the Internet? Do they want weird, sad people like me to go away permanently? Do they think it's a good idea for some people to off themselves? How can you tell when you are one of those people who should slash his wrists the right way with a razor blade? Is there an answer for that too? I Googled but nothing concrete came up. Just ways to complete the mission. Not justification.

Some days I have his parents beat him with clothes hangers and starve him.

Other days his classmates throw him to the ground and kick him until he's wet with blood, at which point they take turns pissing on his head.

Sometimes he suffers from unrequited love and cries every single night alone in his closet clutching a pillow to his chest.

Other times he's abducted by a sadistic psychopath who waterboards him nightly—Guantánamo Bay–style—and deprives him of drinking water during the day while he is forced to sit in a *Clockwork Orange*–type room full of strobe lights, Beethoven symphonies, and horrific images projected on a huge screen.

I don't think anyone else has noticed Herr Silverman's constantly clothed forearms, or if they have, no one has said anything about it in class. I haven't overheard anything in the hallways.

I wonder if I'm really the only one who's noticed, and if so, what does that say about me?

Does that make me weird?

(Or weirder than I already am?)

Or just observant?

So many times I've thought about asking Herr Silverman why he never rolls up his sleeves, but I don't for some reason.[5]

---

5 Sometimes when I stay after class to talk with Herr Silverman about life—while he's trying to put a positive spin on whatever depressing subject I've brought up—I'll pretend I have X-ray vision and stare at his clothed forearms, trying to end the mystery, but it never works because I, unfortunately, don't really have X-ray vision.

Some days he encourages me to write; other days he says I'm "gifted" and then smiles like he's being truthful, and I'll come close to asking him the question about his never-exposed forearms, but I never do, and that seems odd—utterly ridiculous, considering how badly I want to ask and how much the answer could save me.

As if his response will be sacred or life-altering *or something* and I'm saving it for later—like an emotional antibiotic, or a depression lifeboat.

Sometimes I really believe that.

But why?

Maybe my brain's just fucked.

Or maybe I'm terrified that I might be wrong about him and I'm just making things up in my head—that there's nothing under those shirtsleeves at all, and he just likes the look of covered forearms.

It's a fashion statement.

He's more like Linda[6] than I am.

End of story.

I worry Herr Silverman will laugh at me when I ask about his covered forearms.

---

6 Linda is my mother. I call her Linda because it annoys her. She says it "de-moms" her. But she de-mommed herself when she rented an apartment in Manhattan and left me all alone in South Jersey to fend for myself most weeks and increasingly more weekends. She says she needs to be in New York because of her fashion-designing career, but I'm pretty sure it's so she can screw her French boyfriend, Jean-Luc, and keep the hell away from her fucked-up son. She checked out of my life right after the bad shit with Asher went down, maybe because it was too intense for her to handle. I don't know.

He'll make me feel stupid for wondering—hoping—all this time.

That he'll call me a freak.

That he'll think I'm a pervert for thinking about it so much.

That he'll pull an ugly, disgusted face that'll make me feel like he and I could never ever be similar at all, and I'm therefore delusional.

That would kill me, I think.

Do my spirit in for good.

It really would.

And so I've come to worry that my not asking is simply the product of my boundless cowardice.

As I sit there alone at the breakfast table wondering if Linda will remember today's significance, knowing deep down that she's simply not going to call—I decide to instead wonder if the Nazi officer who carried my P-38 in WWII ever dreamed his sidearm would end up as modern art, across the Atlantic Ocean, in New Jersey, seventy-some years later, loaded and ready to kill the closest modern-day equivalent of a Nazi that we have at my high school.

The German who originally owned the P-38—what was his name?

Was he one of the nice Germans Herr Silverman tells us about? The ones who didn't hate Jews or gays or blacks or anyone really but just had the misfortune of being born in Germany during a really fucked time.

Was he anything like me?

FOUR

I have this signature really long dirty-blond hair that hangs over my eyes and past my shoulders. I've been growing it for years, ever since the government came after my dad and he fled the country.[7]

---

7 You won't believe this, but my father was actually a minor rock star back in the early 1990s. His stage name was Jack Walker, which were his two favorite drinks: Jack Daniel's, Johnnie Walker. How clever! Do you know him? *No?* How shocking! You might remember his band, Tether Me Slowly, or the "East Coast's answer to grunge," according to *Rolling Stone,* once upon a time. You've definitely heard his one big hit, "Underwater Vatican," because they play it all the goddamn time on classic-rock radio. He toured with the Jesus Lizard, Pearl Jam, Nirvana, and others as an opening act. Signed a HUGE record deal, had a creative block, became an alcoholic, married my mom, made a crap sophomore album, developed a drug habit (or should I say developed *another* drug habit because—as we learned in health class—alcohol is a drug), was too much of a wuss to OD or off himself like a proper rock star, had me, quit making music, lived off what he made from basically one lucky song and selling his rock 'n' roll paraphernalia on eBay (including the smashed and signed Kurt Cobain guitar that used to hang over my bed), became a has-been one-hit-wonder joke who never even touched a guitar anymore, grew bloated and perpetually red-skinned and unrecognizable, accused Linda of having affairs, began to disappear for days at a time, clandestinely started overnight gambling in Atlantic City, stopped paying taxes, woke his fifteen-year-old son in the middle of the goddamn night to give me his father's WWII souvenirs and knock me out with his roses-and-mustard-gas

And my long locks piss Linda off something awful, especially since she's into contemporary fashion. She says I look like a "grunge-rock stoner"[8] and back when she was still around caring about me, Linda actually made me submit to a drug test—pissing into a cup—which I passed.[9]

I didn't get Linda a good-bye present, and I start to feel guilty about that, so I cut off all my hair with the scissors in the kitchen—the ones we usually use to cut food.

I cut it all down to the scalp in a wild orgy of arms and hands and silver blades.

Then I mash all of my hair into a big ball and wrap it in pink paper.

I'm laughing the whole time.

I cut out a little square of pink paper and write on the back.

Kurt Vonnegut breath, told me to be a good man, told me to take care of Linda, was rumored to have fled by banana fucking cargo boat to some Venezuelan jungle just before the Feds could nab him, and hasn't been heard from since. Every time I hear "Underwater Vatican" now, I want to tear down the walls, and not just because every penny from every royalty check goes to the U.S. government and not me. Linda was pissed about the money she owed the government, all the lawyer shenanigans, losing the big house, the cars, but other than that, she was pretty much like "good fucking riddance" and then her parents died and she inherited enough money to start her NYC designing business and keep me here in South Jersey. My father—whose real name was Ralph Peacock—had Linda sign a prenuptial agreement, I'm certain of that, because no one would have put up with his faded-rock-star shit for so long. But the joke was this: In the end, she got absolutely nothing out of the deal. He was pretty much a bastard. And shitty mom though she may be, Linda still turns heads. She's beautiful—just what you'd think an ex-model would look like in her late thirties.
8 Aka my dad, circa 1991.
9 Like father, unlike son.

Dear Delilah,
Here you go.
You got your wish.
Congratulations!
Love, Samson

I fold the square in half and tape it to the gift, which looks quite odd—almost like I tried to wrap a pocket of air.

Then I stick the present in the refrigerator, which seems hilarious.

Linda will be looking for a chilled bottle of Riesling to calm her jangled nerves after getting the news about her son ridding the world of Asher Beal and Leonard Peacock too.

She'll find the pink wrap job.

Linda will wonder about my allusion to *Samson and Delilah* when she reads the card, because that was the title of my father's failed sophomore record, but will get the joke just as soon as she opens her present.

I imagine her clutching her chest, faking the tears, playing the victim, and being all dramatic.

Jean-Luc will really have his professionally manicured French hands full.

No sex for him maybe, or maybe not.

Maybe their affair will blossom without me around to psychologically anchor poor Linda to reality and maternal duties.

Maybe once I'm gone, she'll float away to France like a shiny new silver little-kid birthday balloon.

She'll probably even lose a dress size without me around to trigger her "stress eating."

Maybe Linda won't return to our house ever again.

Maybe she and Jean-Luc will go to the fashion capital of the world, the City of Light, *auw-hauh-hauw!*, and screw like bunnies happily ever after.

She'll sell everything, and the new homeowners will find my hair in the refrigerator and be like *What the ... ?*

My hair'll just end up in the trash and that will be that.

Gone.

Forgotten.

RIP, hair.

Or maybe they'll donate my locks to one of those wig-making places that help out kids with cancer. Like my hair would get a second shot at life with a little innocent-hearted bald chemo girl maybe.

I'd like that.

I really would.

My hair deserves it.

So I'm really hoping for that cancer-kid-helping outcome if Linda goes to France without coming home first, or maybe even Linda will donate my hair.

Anything's possible, I guess.

I stare at the mirror over the kitchen sink.[10]

---

10 Linda needs mirrors more than she needs oxygen, so there are mirrors in every goddamn room of our house.

The no-hair guy staring back at me looks so strange now.

He's like a different person with all uneven patches on his scalp.

He looks thinner.

I can see his cheekbones sticking out where his blond curtains used to hang.

How long has this guy been hiding under my hair?

I don't like him.

"I'm going to kill you later today," I say to that guy in the mirror, and he just smiles back at me like he can't wait.

"Promise?" I hear someone say, which freaks me out, because my lips didn't move.

I mean—it wasn't me who said, "Promise?"

It's like there's a voice trapped inside the glass.

So I stop looking in the mirror.

Just for good measure, I smash that mirror with a coffee mug, because I don't want the mirror me to speak ever again.

Shards rain down into the sink and then a million little mes look up like so many tiny minnows.

FIVE

I'm already late for school, but I need to stop at my next-door-neighbor Walt's[11] so that I can give him his present.

Today, I knock once and let myself into Walt's house because he has to walk slowly with one of those gray-piped four-footed walkers that has dirty tennis balls attached to

---

11 I met Walt during a blizzard, just after we moved into the new house. I remember Linda asking me to shovel the driveway, even though it was still snowing, because she had to go out to meet another fake designer or some bulimic model or whomever. I think she was trying to "cure" me by assigning manly tasks because of what happened with Asher and me, even though she refused to believe me when I tried to tell her what happened because she's a selfish, oblivious bitch. And on that snow day, shoveling was an impossible task, because just as soon as I got one shovel width done, new snow had already covered the cleared driveway once more. It took me hours, and I was exhausted by the time Linda said, "Good enough." I was just about to go inside when she asked me to make sure our neighbor was okay. "He's an old man. Ask him if he needs his driveway shoveled or anything else," Linda said, which was strange because she's not usually considerate—or even aware—of anyone but herself. Again, I think she was trying to "cure" me without addressing what happened. When I didn't move, Linda said, "Go, Leo. Be a good neighbor. We want to make the right sort of impression. Especially after all that's happened." So I walked through a few feet of snow as Linda pulled out of the driveway. I had planned on just going inside our new home once she had driven away, but she idled in the street, watching me through the falling snow. Just as soon as I rang the doorbell, she drove away. When no one

protect his hardwood floors. It's difficult for him to get around, especially with bad lungs, so he just gave me a key and said, "Come in whenever you feel like it. And come often!"

He's been smoking since he was twelve, and I've been helping him buy his Pall Mall Reds on the Internet to save money. The first time, I found this phenomenal deal: two hundred cigarettes for nineteen dollars, and he proclaimed me a hero right then and there. He doesn't even have a

---

answered I thought I was in luck, but then I heard yelling inside and what sounded like gunshots. It shook me right out of the quiet winter scene I was in and got my heart going even more than it already was. I waited for a second, thinking I might be hearing things, but then I heard more gunshots, so I pulled out my cell phone and called the police. Three cop cars arrived a few minutes later with their sirens blaring and their lights flashing. They had this bullhorn and they used it to tell me to step away from the house. So I did. One of the cops went up to the door with his gun drawn and knocked really hard. No one answered. So he trudged through the snow toward the back of the house. He looked in all the windows. A minute or so later, the front door opened and an old man stood there leaning on a walker. "What the hell is going on?" he said. "Sir, there was a report of gunshots. Are you okay?" the police officer said. "I'm just watching a Bogart movie, for Christ's sake." The cops looked at me like they were pissed and then we all went inside to sort out the facts. Once the cops were satisfied that it was all just a misunderstanding, they left. "What were you even doing at my front door?" the old man said to me. "My mom wanted to know if you needed your driveway shoveled. That's how this all started. I'm sorry I called the police. But the gunshots sounded real." The old man smiled proudly and said, "That's my new surround-sound system. They're redoing the sound on most of the old films, and I can't hear so good, so I turn it up. You ever watch good old Humphrey Bogart in action?" "No," I said. He opened his eyes so wide and said, "Jesus Christ, you have no idea what you're missing! Get your uneducated ass in my living room and we'll start with *The Treasure of the Sierra Madre*." And that's how Linda passed me off to the next-door neighbor when I needed a father figure—when I first started getting fucked in the head. Watching old movies with Walt seemed like a strange thing to do on a snow day, but it beat shoveling, so I followed him into his living room, declined the cigarette he offered me, heard Bogart say, "Will you stake a fellow American to a meal?" and just sort of settled in for what would turn out to be hours and days and weeks of black-and-white movies.

computer in his home, let alone the Internet. So it was like I performed a miracle, getting cigarettes that cheap delivered to his doorstep, because he was paying a hell of a lot more at the local convenience store. I've been bringing over my laptop—our Internet signal reaches his living room—and we've been searching for the best deals every week. He's always trying to give me half of what he saves, but I never take his money.[12]

It's funny because he's rich,[13] but always keen on finding a bargain. Maybe that's why he's rich. I don't know.

A "helper" comes and takes care of him most days, but not until nine thirty AM, so it's always just Walt and me before school.

"Walt?" I say as I walk through the smoky hallway, under the crystal chandelier, toward the smoky living room where he usually sleeps surrounded by overflowing ashtrays and empty bottles. "Walt?"

I find him in his La-Z-Boy, smoking a Pall Mall Red, eyes bloodshot from drinking scotch last night.

His robe isn't shut, so I can see his naked, hairless chest. It's the pinkish-red sunset color of conch-shell innards.

---

12 Maybe you think I'm an asshole, making smoking more affordable for an old man with shot lungs? I'm not a big fan of smoking, for the record, even though I'm about to commit suicide. Irony? But Walt pretty much has old-time movies, cigarettes, scotch, and me. Cigarettes are 25 percent of his life. So I don't judge him for smoking. Why should he want to extend his life longer? He started before they even knew it was bad for you, so maybe his addiction isn't really his fault anyway. Maybe if I were born eighty-some years ago, I'd be addicted to cigarettes too.

13 Seventy-inch flat-screen TV; Oriental rugs; garage-kept brand-new Mercedes-Benz, which he never even drives; professionally landscaped yard; in-ground sprinkler system; original Norman Rockwell painting in the hallway—you get the picture.

He looks at me with his best black-and-white movie-star face[14] and says, "You despise me, don't you?"

It's a line from *Casablanca*, which we've watched together a million times.

Standing next to his chair with my backpack between my feet, I answer with Rick's follow-up line in the film, saying, "If I gave you any thought I probably would."

Then I follow it with a line from *The Big Sleep*, saying, "My, my, my. Such a lot of guns around town and so few brains," which feels pretty cool and authentic considering I have the Nazi P-38 in my backpack.

Walt counters with a line from *Key Largo*, saying, "You were right. When your head says one thing and your whole life says another, your head always loses."

I smile even bigger because whenever we trade Bogart-related quotes, our conversations seem to make a weird sort of sense that is unpredictable and almost poetic.

I go with a Bogart quote I looked up on the Internet, "There never seems to be any trouble brewing around a bar until a woman puts that high heel over the brass rail. Don't ask me why, but somehow women at bars seem to create trouble among men."

He goes back to the *Casablanca* well and says, "Where were you last night?"

---

14 If you took away all his wrinkles and rogue white hair, he'd look like a seasoned George Clooney.

So I finish the quote, playing Rick and say, "That's so long ago, I don't remember."

He says, "Will I see you tonight?"

It sort of freaks me out, because no one will ever see me again after today, so the question seems weighty. I remind myself that he couldn't possibly know my plan; he's just playing the dumb Bogart game we always play. He's clueless.

I become Rick again and finish the quote: "I never make plans that far ahead."

Walt smiles, blows smoke at the ceiling, and says, "Louis, I think this is the beginning of a beautiful friendship."

I sit down on his couch and end the game the way we always do by saying, "Here's looking at you, kid."

"Why aren't you in school learning?" Walt says as the flame from his Zippo lights up his face and another cigarette sparks to life. But he doesn't really care. I skip school all the time just to watch old Bogart films with him. He loves it when I skip school.

He starts coughing and you can hear the terrible tobacco phlegm rattling.

A two-pack-a-day sixty-year-habit smoker's cough.

Foul.

I just stare at Walt for a long time, waiting for him to wipe his hand on his robe and catch his breath.

I wish he were healthier, but it's hard to imagine him without a cigarette in his hand. Like I bet even in his high school yearbook pictures he was smoking. That's just who he is. Like Bogart too.

Man, I'm going to miss Walt so much. Watching old smoky Bogart movies with him is one of the few things I'll truly miss. It was always the highlight of my week.

Walt says, "You okay, Leonard? You don't look well."

I shake off the weirdness, wipe my eyes with my sleeve, and say, "Yeah, I'm fine."

He says, "You got all your hair tucked up into that fedora along with the tops of your ears?"[15]

I nod.

I don't want to tell him I cut off all my hair, for some reason, maybe because Walt's one of my best friends—he really cares about me, I swear to god—and he'd know something was wrong if he saw my fucked-up haircut. He'd get upset, and I want to exit on a good note—I want this to be a happy good-bye, something he can remember and actually feel good about after I'm gone.

"Bought you a present," I say, and then pull the turtle-looking wrap job from the top of my backpack.

He says, "It's not my birthday, you know."

I hope he guesses that it's mine—or that he might figure it out, deduce it, so I wait a second as he fingers the present and tries to mentally guess what the hell it might be.

He looks so happy to get a present.

I kind of promise myself that I won't kill Asher Beal, nor

---

15 He's talking about my Bogart hat, which is too big and even covers my eyebrows. It's kind of ridiculous.

will I off myself, if only Walt just says "happy birthday" to me one time, as silly and trivial as that seems.

He doesn't, and that makes me sad, even though I probably never even told him when my birthday was and I know he would definitely say "happy birthday" if I had.

But I really want him to say "happy birthday" to me without any prompting, and when he doesn't, I get to feeling hollow as a dry-docked boat or something.

"Why do I get pink paper? Do you think I'm a faggot?" he says, and then starts laughing really hard and coughing again.

I say, "It's the twenty-first century. Don't be such a homophobe," but I'm not really mad at him.

Walt's so old that you can't hold his bigotry against him, because for almost all his life it was okay for him to say "faggot" among friends, and then suddenly it wasn't.

He also says things like *nigger* and *kike* and *Polack* and *chink* and *light in the loafers* and *sand nigger* and *slant* and *spade* and *spook* and *camel jockey* and *smokes* and *porch monkey* and just about a trillion other awful slurs.

I hate bigotry, but I also love Walt.

It's like Herr Silverman teaches us about the Nazis. Maybe Walt was just unlucky being born at a time when everyone was prejudiced against homosexuals and minorities, and that's just the way it was for his generation. I don't know.

I'm starting to get sad about all that, so I change the subject by pointing at his present and saying, "Well, aren't you going to open it?"

He nods once like a little kid and then tears into the pink paper with his yellow shaky fingers. Halfway in he says, "I think I know what this is!"

When he has the Bogart hat unwrapped, he says, "Hot digitty dog!" all corny and nestles the hat down on his white hair.

It's a perfect fit, just like I knew it would be, because I measured his head once when he was passed out, drunk.

He composes his face, gets all black-and-white-movie-star-looking, and says, "I've got a job to do too. Where I'm going you can't follow. What I've got to do, you can't be any part of. Leonard, I'm no good at being noble but it doesn't take much to see that the problems of three little people don't amount to a hill of beans in this crazy world. Someday you'll understand that."

I smile because he switched my name in for Ilsa's. He does that sometimes when doing lines from *Casablanca*.[16]

He smiles back real nice and says, "Wow. My very own Bogart hat. I love it!"

_____

16 Maybe you're wondering why a teenager in 2011 likes watching Bogart films with an old man? Good question. At first, it was just something to do, somewhere to be where I felt wanted, because Walt's pretty lonely. But I really grew to get, understand, and love Bogart Hollywood land. Walt says the movies were for men who came home from World War II disoriented, trying to make sense of the new postwar world, trying to relearn how to be men in a new domesticated life with women. There were no women around during the fighting overseas, just men supporting men, which is the reason for the Lauren Bacall–type femme fatales. During the war, men forgot how to interact with and trust women. And I like the fact that Walt takes me to a place none of my classmates even know exists. I admire Bogart because he does what's right regardless of consequences—even when the consequences are stacked high against him—unlike just about everyone else in my life.

And then I just start lying and can't stop myself no matter how hard I try.

I don't know why I do it.

Maybe to keep myself from crying, because I can feel the tears coming on strong—like there's a thunderstorm in my skull that's about to break.

So I tell him I got the hat off the Internet on a site that auctions old movie props. All proceeds go toward curing smoker's cough and throat cancer, which killed good old unkillable Humphrey Bogart. I say the hat Walt's wearing right at this very moment was the same hat Humphrey Bogart wore while playing Sam Spade in *The Maltese Falcon*.

His eyes open really wide, and then Walt gets this sad look on his face, like he knows I'm lying when I don't have to—like he loves the hat even if it's *not* a movie prop, even if I found it on the street or something, and I know that too, that I don't have to make shit up because what we have as friends is real and true already—but I just keep telling mistruths and he doesn't want to call me on it; he doesn't want to make me feel shameful and fuck up the good moment that is happening.

That sad look on his face just makes me say things like "really" and "I swear to god" like I do sometimes when I am lying.

I say, "It's really really Bogart's hat, I swear to god. *Really*. Just don't tell my mom about this because I had to spend some serious money—like upwards of twenty-five grand I debited from her Visa card, which all goes to cancer research, all of it—and I had to get the hat just so that we might have a little piece of Bogie history, just so we might at least have that forever. Right?"

I feel so awful, because the truth is that I bought the hat at the thrift store for four dollars and fifty cents.

Walt's eyes look all glazey and distant, like I shot him with the P-38.

"So do you like it?" I ask. "Do you like owning Bogie's hat? Does wearing it make you feel tough and capable of saving the day?"

Walt smiles real sad, makes his Bogie face, and says, "What have you ever given me besides money? You ever given me any of your confidence, any of the truth? Haven't you tried to buy my loyalty with money and nothing else?"

I recognize the quote. It's from *The Maltese Falcon*. So I finish it by saying, "What else is there I can buy you with?"

We look at each other in our Bogart hats and it's like we're communicating, even though we're completely silent.

I'm trying to let him know what I'm about to do.

I'm hoping he can save me, even though I realize he can't.

His Bogie hat is gray with a black band and really looks like Sam Spade's. It was a lucky thrift store find. It really was. Like Walt was destined to have this very hat.

I remember this other weirdly appropriate quote from *The Maltese Falcon* and so I say, "I haven't lived a good life. I've been bad. Worse than you could know."

But Walt doesn't play along this time. He gets real twitchy

and nervous and then he starts asking me why I gave him the hat at this particular juncture—"Why *today*?"—and—"Why do you look so sad all of a sudden?"—and—"What's wrong?"

Then he starts asking me to take off my hat, asking if I cut my hair, and when I don't answer he asks me if I've talked to my mother today—if she's been around lately.

I say, "I really have to go to school now. You're a fantastic neighbor, Walt. Really. Almost like a father to me. No need to worry."

I'm fighting the big-time tears again, so I turn my back on him and walk out through the smoky hallway, under the crystal chandelier, out of Walt's life forever.

The whole time he yells, "Leonard. Leonard, wait! Let's talk. I'm really worried about you. What's going on? Why don't you stay awhile? Please. Take a day off. We can watch a Bogie movie. Things will seem better. Bogart always—"

I open the front door and pause long enough to hear him coughing and hacking as he tries to chase me, using his sad drugstore tennis-ball walker.

He could die today, I think, *he really could.*

And then I just stride out of his house knowing that it was the perfect way to say good-bye to Walt. My storming out right at that very moment was like the emotional climax of an old-school Bogart film. In my mind, I could even hear the stringed instruments building to a dramatic crescendo.

"Good-bye, Walt," I say as I stride toward my high school.

SIX
LETTER FROM THE FUTURE NUMBER 1

Dear First Lieutenant Leonard,

Billy Penn is doing his best Jesus imitation.

That's what you'll say today when you get here and report for duty.

That'll be in about twenty years and one hour from where you are in the present moment, roughly thirteen months after you decide to risk entering into the great, open, no-longer-civilized void.

Like me, you'll decide that life on crowded, premium dry land—where you have to elbow everyone out of the way just for a breath of fresh air—is not for you.

And you would never live like a rodent in tube city, now would you?

Inevitably, you'll come join me in what we now call Outpost 37, Lighthouse 1—what you currently know as Philadelphia, the Comcast Center skyscraper.

These days, tides rise and fall by hundreds of feet due to the increased speeds of weather patterns and the daily earthquakes that open and close gigantic underwater crevasses. Our planet is re-forming.

Today the water is so low, we can see Billy Penn's feet and just a few inches of the old City Hall building atop of which he is still perched. City Hall is under the sea so it looks like Billy Penn's walking on water, hence your Jesus reference.

Greetings from the future.

The year is 2032.

There's been a nuclear holocaust, just like everyone feared there would be, and we've managed to melt the polar ice caps, which flooded the planet, covering a third of all known land with sea. Remember that movie your science teacher showed you? Well, Al Gore was right.

The nukes wiped out a fourth of the world's population, and a food shortage from lack of land and fresh water took care of another fourth, or so they say.

Here in the North American Land Collective—we merged with Canada and Mexico several years ago—our overall losses weren't as dramatic as in other parts of the world, but our land loss was just as great. This resulted in what has been compared to a migratory heart attack. Everyone was forced into the middle of our country, which caused chaos, of course, and required military law and a new sort of totalitarian government.

They've started to build vertically. Sky is the new frontier, the hot real estate. It's all elevators and sky-scrapers and enclosed tubeways in the clouds. People mostly live their lives indoors, somewhere between the earth and outer space, hardly ever breathing unfiltered air or feeling direct sunlight on their bare skin. They're like gerbils in plastic-tubing cage cities.

But not us.

We have volunteered to man Outpost 37, Lighthouse 1, and we spend most of our days boating around the tops of what was once the Philadelphia skyline. Including you, there are only four of us here.

It is our job to provide light for any vessels that might accidentally find their way into our sector, so they will not crash into the exposed tops of under-water skyscrapers. We are to aid in military operations, of course, but we have not seen another human or a single boat of any kind in more than a year. We have not been officially contacted by the North American Land Collective government in ninety-seven days, nor have we been able to make our satellite links, which leads us to believe that all global communications have been shut down.

Why?

We don't know.

But here's the kicker: We do not care.

We are happy.

We are self-sufficient, stocked with twenty more years' worth of poly-frozen food packets.

Scientists have proved that being exposed to so much unfiltered air, being closer to the great nuclear fallout clouds that drift aimlessly across Global Common Area Two, or what you call the Atlantic Ocean, will definitely shorten our lives quicker than smoking two packs of cigarettes a day, and yet we are at peace with our position and feel as though we have escaped—or maybe like we have finally arrived home.

We're living in the moment.

Sometimes we feel guilty knowing that so many people have suffered through the horrors that put us here, but as we had no control over those things, we simply try to enjoy our good fortune.

Our life is strange.

We spend our days in the boats searching the tops of skyscrapers for anything interesting, entering apartments and offices and stores as amateur archaeologists. These are the Egyptian pyramids of our time—"our underwater Machu Picchu," you like to say.

You excavate more with the others, "reconstructing the lives of strangers." It's like a game. "Our greatest form of entertainment." The three of you love to play Who Lived Here? and your answers are full of heroes and heroines who once did brave and noble deeds back before the sea swallowed up their entire civilization.

There are a trillion stories to be found beneath us. "Outpost 37 is perhaps the greatest interactive fiction library man has ever known."

You said that, by the way.

I'm always quoting the future you.

You're quite quotable.

You also love spotting dolphins. There is a large school of them here. They've begun to mutate due to the nuclear fallout and are slightly larger than they used to be. You often ride on their backs and call them buses. "I'm going to catch a bus," you'll say to S and she'll clap and laugh as you hop onto one, holding the fin, being sprayed by the creature's breath. We treat them like pets, swim with them often, and cut off the red squidlike parasites whenever the dolphins roll and offer up their smooth white bellies.

One youngster swims alongside your boat every morning when you make rounds. You named him Horatio, because he's so loyal. We joke about him being your best friend and call you Hamlet, a play you are still reading nightly after all these years. "It gives and gives," you say. Just like your high school English teacher told you.

But your favorite thing to do is scuba diving down into the city, exploring the watery streets that are still full of cars and hot dog stands and monuments and park benches and petrified trees and sports complexes and so many other things from our past, your present.

We only have so many bottles of oxygen in storage, so you don't get to go as often as you'd like, because you are saving a few for the future. Rationing. You believe in the future now. It's easy for you, because you love the present. Also, because you have S now.

You still get melancholy sometimes, especially when you think about the past, but mostly you are happy.

It's a good, weird life.

We are a happy little family.

I understand that you are going through a tough time, Leonard. We've talked about it in detail during our late nights manning the great beam of light.

Your past—what you are currently experiencing— would be hard for anyone to endure. You've been so strong, making it this far. I admire your courage, and hope you can hold out a little longer. Twenty years seems like a long time to you, I bet, but it will pass quicker than you can ever imagine.

I know you really want to kill that certain someone. That you feel abandoned by your parents. Let down by your school.

Alone.

Peerless.

Trapped.

Afraid.

I know that you really just want everything to end—that you can't see anything good in your future, that the world looks dark and terrible, and maybe you're right—the world can definitely be a dreadful place.

I know you're just barely holding it together.

But please hold on a little longer.

For us.

For yourself.

You are going to absolutely love Outpost 37.

You're going to be the keeper of the light.

My first lieutenant.

Our beam is quite impressive, even if no one ever sees it but us—we send it out every night religiously. And when we turn out the lighthouse to conserve power, you will see stars like you've never seen before.

Mind-boggling stars, the depths of which you will never map.

A strange, beautiful new world awaits, Leonard.

We've found an oasis in their ruins. We really have.

You want to see it, so just hold on, okay?

With much hope for the future (and from a man who knows for certain!),

Commander E

SEVEN

My school is shaped like an empty box with no lid.

There's this very beautiful courtyard in the center, with four squares of grass, benches, cobblestone sidewalks that make a huge +, with White House–looking columns at the far end, and a cupola tower that overlooks the whole thing.

Before school or during lunch periods it's crawling with students—like an awful cockroach infestation of teenagers. But during classes it's serene, and I can never resist sitting down on a bench and watching clouds and birds fly by overhead.

I like to pretend I'm a prisoner kept in a dark, dank cell who's only allowed fifteen minutes a day in the yard, so that I remember to really enjoy looking up. And that's what I'm doing when Vice Principal Torres taps me on the shoulder and says, "I hate to interrupt the nice moment you're having, but shouldn't you be in class, Mr. Peacock?"

I start to laugh because he's acting all superior like he

always does. He has no idea that I have the P-38 on me, that I could shoot him in the heart and end his life right now just by pulling a trigger, and therefore he has no power over me at all.

He says, "What's so funny?"

And I feel so fucking mighty knowing that the P-38 is loaded in my backpack, so I say, "Nothing at all. Care to sit down? Beautiful day. *Beautiful.* You look stressed. Maybe you should take a rest with me. Looking up at the sky is really healthy. I learned that by watching afternoon television aimed at women. Let's chat. Let's try to understand each other. What do you say?"

He just looks at me for a second and then says, "What's with the hat?"

I say, "Been watching Bogie films with my neighbor. I've become quite a fan."

When he doesn't answer, I say, "You know—Humphrey Bogart? *Here's looking at you, kid?*"

He says, "I know who Humphrey Bogart is. Now back to class."

I cross my legs to let him know that I'm not afraid of him, and then say, "I missed homeroom and haven't checked in yet at the office, so technically I'm on my own time. Haven't punched in, so to speak, boss. Not yet under your jurisdiction. Right now, I'm just an everyman in a park."

Vice Principal Torres's face starts to turn eggplant purple as he says, "I don't have time for double talk this morning, Leonard."

So I say, "I'm talking pretty effectively, I think. I've answered all of your questions honestly and accurately. I'm always straight with you. But you don't listen. *No one listens.* Why don't you just sit down? It'll make you feel better. It could really—"

"Leonard," he says. "Enough."

I say, "*Jeez,*" because I was really trying to make a connection. I would have talked with him openly and honestly—no double talk at all—if he would have just sat down, taken a few minutes to be human.

What's so important that he couldn't take five minutes to look up at the sky with me?

Then Vice Principal Torres does this really lame, unoriginal thing, which depresses me. He probably does this bit with his son, Nathan, whose elementary school picture[17] is on VP Torres's desk. Vice Principal Torres says, "Mr. Peacock, I'm going to count to three, and if you're not on your way to class by the time I say three, you're going to have a big problem."

"What type of problem am I going to have?"

He raises his index finger and says, "One."

"Don't you think we should discuss the consequence of my possible inaction so I can decide whether or not doing what you have requested is truly in my best interest? I want to make an informed decision. I want to think. This is school

---

17 Turtleneck sweater. Missing-tooth smile. Bowl cut. Cute kid.

after all. Aren't you supposed to encourage us to think? Help me out here."

He makes a peace sign, and says, "Two."

I look up at the sky, smile, and then stand just before he says three, only because I need to shoot Asher Beal. That's the only reason. I swear to god. I don't want to make this day any harder than it will already be. I'm not afraid of Vice Principal Torres, his fingers, or his lame-ass counting. I assure you.

I start to walk to the office, but then I spin around and say, "I'm worried about you, Vice Principal Torres. You seem stressed. And it's affecting your work."

He says, "I've got a full slate today. Cut me a break, okay? Will you just go to class, Mr. Peacock? *Please.*"

I nod once and, as I walk toward the main office, I hear Vice Principal Torres sigh loudly. I don't think his sigh is directed at me so much as it's directed at his life—the fact that he's so stressed and busy.

It's like all the adults I know absolutely hate their jobs and their lives too. I don't think I know anyone over eighteen who wouldn't be better off dead, besides Walt[18] and Herr Silverman, and knowing that makes me feel confident about what I'm about to do later on today.

---

18 Who is, ironically, dying.

EIGHT

I do this thing sometimes where I put on this black suit I have for formal occasions such as funerals and I carry this crazy empty briefcase I got at the thrift store. Only I don't go to school.

I practice being an adult, like I pretend I'm going to a job.

I walk toward the train station, and about two blocks away from it I always fall in line with other suits swinging briefcases.

I've studied their dead expressions enough to blend in.

I walk soldierlike, copying their steps, swinging my empty briefcase just so—almost goose-stepping.

I insert the coins into the bins outside the station and grab an old-fashioned paper newspaper, which I tuck under my arm, just to blend in.

I pay for my ticket at the machine.

I descend using the escalator.

And then I stand around all zombie-faced waiting for the train to come.

I know this will sound wrong, but whenever I wear my funeral suit, go to the train station, and pretend I have a job in the city, it always makes me think about the Nazi trains that took the World War II Jews to the death camps. What Herr Silverman taught us about. I know that's a horrible and maybe even offensive comparison, but waiting there on the platform, among the suits, I feel like I'm just waiting to go to some horrible place where everything good ends and then misery ensues forever and ever and ever—which reminds me of the awful stories we learned in Holocaust class, whether it's offensive or not.

I mean we won World War II, right?

And yet all of these adults—the sons and daughters and grandchildren of our World War II heroes—get on metaphorical death trains anyway, even though we beat the Nazi fascists a long time ago and, therefore, every American is free to do anything at all here in this supposedly great free country. Why don't they use their freedom and liberty to pursue happiness?

When the train comes, the herd jumps on really quickly—like they've all been underwater forever and there's oxygen inside.

No one talks.

It's always quiet.

No music or anything like that.

No one says, "How was your night?" or, "What are your dreams and aspirations?" Or tells jokes or whistles or does anything at all to lighten the mood and make the morning commute more bearable.

I think about how I strongly dislike all the kids at my school, but at least they'd seem alive if they were on the train. They'd be cracking jokes and laughing and feeling each other up and planning parties and talking about the stupid shit they watched on TV last night and texting each other and singing pop songs and doodling maybe and a million other things.

But these adults in suits just sit there or stand and sometimes grimly read the paper, angrily poke smartphone screens, sip tongue-scorching coffee from disposable cups, and barely even blink.

Observing them gets me so down; it makes me feel like I never want to be an adult. That my decision to use the P-38 is for the best. That I'm escaping some horrible fate and I'm like the Jews who killed their sons and daughters before the Nazi soldiers could take them away to the experimentation torture camps.

Herr Silverman once had us write an essay in first person from the point of view of a Jewish person during the Holocaust. I wrote about a Jewish father who killed his wife and kids and then himself to avoid being taken to the concentration camps, which was a pretty bleak exercise, but an easy essay for me to write actually. The Jewish father I wrote about was a good man who loved his family—he loved them so much he wouldn't allow them to experience the Nazi horrors.

My essay was mostly an apology letter. My anonymous narrator wrote it as a prayer, asking his god's forgiveness for what he had to do. That essay turned out exceptionally authentic. Herr Silverman even read parts aloud to the class and said I was "empathetic" beyond my years.

I heard other kids in my class whisper all sorts of things about me afterward, saying that I had justified killing children and suicide, but my classmates just didn't get it, because they are spoiled teenagers living here in America at the beginning of the twenty-first century. They've never had to make any real decisions at all. Their lives are easy and unremarkable. They're not awake.

Herr Silverman is always asking us if we realize how much of our lives are dictated by the fact that we were born in America eighteen years ago, and what would we really have done if we were German kids during World War II when Hitler Youth was all the rage?

Me—I'm honest enough to admit I don't know.

My idiot classmates all say they would have defied the Nazis, assassinated Hitler with their bare hands even, when they don't even have the balls or brains to defy our lame-ass flunky teachers and robotic parents.

Sheep.

Example: Herr Silverman does this mind-fuck thing where he says to the class, "You are all more or less wearing the same types of clothes—look around the room and you will see it's true. Now imagine you're the only one not wearing a cool symbol. How would that make you feel? The Nike swoop, the three Adidas stripes, the little Polo player on a horse, the Hollister seagull, the symbols of Philadelphia's professional sports teams, even our high school mascot that you athletes wear to battle other schools—some of you wear our Mustang to class even when there is no sporting event scheduled. These are your symbols, what you wear to prove that your identity matches the identity of others. Much like the Nazis had their swastika. We have a very loose dress code here and yet most of you pretty much dress the same. Why? Perhaps you feel it's important not to stray too far from the norm. Would you not also wear a government symbol if it became important and normal to do so? If it were marketed the right way? If it was stitched on the most expensive brand at the mall? Worn by movie stars? The president of the United States?"

It's this type of revolutionary shit Herr Silverman says that always gets the stupid kids in my class angry, red-faced, even ready to fistfight him sometimes, because they don't realize that our teacher is just trying to get them to think. He's not really saying that wearing name-brand clothing is evil. Or that buying Polo clothes makes you a Nazi. Or that wearing a Phillies cap is one step away from fascism.

But it makes me laugh every time because I don't wear any of that name-brand crap, don't play or follow popular sports at all, and wouldn't be found dead wearing our shitty school mascot. I'm not a follower. Not a joiner. I'm not even on Facebook.

So whenever Herr Silverman brings up symbols, I can watch the others squirm and defend without feeling like a damn hypocrite.

Maybe I've transcended my age, so to speak.

My classmates are all repressed monkeys.

NINE

In my funeral suit, on the train, pretending to be a workaday Tom, I always pick out a target—the saddest-looking person I can find—and then I'll get off at whatever stop the target does and follow.

Ninety-nine percent of the time the target's so comatose the target doesn't even notice me.

I'll trail the target, hanging five or so feet behind, and the target will always walk really quickly because the target is forever late and in a rush to get to a job the target inevitably hates, which I just don't get.[19]

---

19 Like Linda, who claims to LOVE LOVE LOVE designing clothing but never misses a chance to complain about and stress over her work. How can she love something that makes her so unhappy—that keeps her away from her only son? Maybe being stressed about work and complaining all the time are a welcome respite from being Leonard Peacock's mom? I don't know. But thinking about that makes me sad. Especially since she became a fashion designer right after I tried to tell her about the bad stuff that happened with Asher. It was like my failed confession drove her away from me—made me repugnant.

The whole time I pretend I have mental telepathy. And with my mind only, I'll say—or think?—to the target, "Don't do it. Don't go to that job you hate. Do something you love today. Ride a roller coaster. Swim in the ocean naked. Go to the airport and get on the next flight to anywhere just for the fun of it. Maybe stop a spinning globe with your finger and then plan a trip to that very spot; even if it's in the middle of the ocean you can go by boat. Eat some type of ethnic food you've never even heard of. Stop a stranger and ask her to explain her greatest fears and her secret hopes and aspirations in detail and then tell her you care because she is a human being. Sit down on the sidewalk and make pictures with colorful chalk. Close your eyes and try to see the world with your nose—allow smells to be your vision. Catch up on your sleep. Call an old friend you haven't seen in years. Roll up your pant legs and walk into the sea. See a foreign film. Feed squirrels. *Do anything! Something!* Because you start a revolution one decision at a time, with each breath you take. Just don't go back to that miserable place you go every day. Show me it's possible to be an adult and also be happy. Please. This is a free country. You don't have to keep doing this if you don't want to. You can do anything you want. Be anyone you want. That's what they tell us at school, but if you keep getting on that train and going to the place you hate I'm going to start thinking the people at school are liars like the Nazis who told the Jews they were just being relocated to work factories. Don't do that to us. Tell us the truth. If adulthood is working some death-camp job you hate for the rest of your life, divorcing your secretly criminal husband, being disappointed in your son, being stressed and miserable, and dating a poser[20] and pretending he's a hero when he's really a lousy person and anyone can tell that just by shaking his slimy hand[21]—if it doesn't get any better, I need to know right now. Just tell me. Spare me from some awful fucking fate. Please."

I'll do the mental telepathy bit for about ten minutes or so as the target climbs out of the subway stop and navigates skyscraper shadows and finally disappears inside a building that usually has a security guard to keep crazy people like me out.[22]

So then I just go to the nearest park, sit with the pigeons, and stare at clouds until my workday is over and it's time to ride home with all the other weary workaday Toms and Jennys, who look even more miserable on the PM return trip.

The rides home always deepen my depression, because these people are free—off work, headed back to families they

---

20 Who probably screws hundreds of other women behind your back, because he's a powerful player in the fashion business, so he definitely can. And people who value fashion first and foremost are not usually humanitarians or Nobel Peace Prize candidates, after all.

21 Herr Silverman said that the Jewish women in the Nazi death camps were often forced to have sex with Nazi officers (maybe like the one who owned my P-38?) just to stay alive and get privileges for themselves and family members. And hearing that made me wonder if Linda has to perform sex acts for Jean-Luc to keep her fashion career alive. (Herr Silverman also said that some sex slaves were teenage kids just like us.)

22 Interesting that businesses in the city have security guards but my high school doesn't. Maybe it will after today. But why protect adults and not children?

chose and made themselves—and yet they still don't look happy.

I always wonder if that's what Linda looks like riding home from New York City in a car—so utterly miserable, zombie-faced, cheated.

Does she look like the mother of a monster?

TEN

I've taken dozens of practice-adulthood days, followed so many suits, but only once did anyone notice me.

It was this beautiful woman wearing huge 1970s sunglasses on the train, even though most of the ride is underground. I could see her mascara running down her cheek, but she was really beautiful otherwise. Like, I was sort of attracted to her.

Long, bright blond hair.

Red lipstick.

Black stockings.

Gray pinstriped skirt suit.

You could tell that she was an authority figure just by the way she sat and dared anyone to say anything about the runny mascara. The vibe she sent out was menacing and it definitely said, "Don't fuck with me."

Regardless, on that day, this woman was by far the most miserable person on the train. You could tell she was upset, but it also looked like she'd rip your face off if you said anything to her.

All the other adults pretended not to notice, which seemed cowardly.

As she was the obvious target for the day, I got off at her stop and followed.

I remember the sound of her high heels clicking on the concrete like cap guns firing.

She walked up the escalator; I did too, trying hard to keep up.

When we cleared the turnstile I started the mental telepathy, saying (or thinking?), "Don't do it. Don't go to that job you hate. Go skydiving. Buy a star on the Internet. Adopt a cat." And I continued with my routine for a city block or so. She turned into a back alley, and when we were halfway down it, she spun around tornadolike and pointed a can of Mace at my nose.

"Who are you and why are you following me?" she said. "I will destroy your day. This is top-grade stuff too. Illegal in the United States. I squeeze this trigger and you won't be able to see for months. You might go blind."

I didn't know what to say, so I put my hands up in the air, like I've seen criminals do in the movies whenever they want to surrender, when some tough Bogart-type guy points a gun and says, "Reach for the sky."

It surprised her, and she took a step back, but she didn't spray me.

"How old are you?" she said.

I said, "I'm seventeen."

"What's your name?"

"Leonard Peacock."

"That's a fake name if I ever heard one."

I said, "I can show you my school ID."

She said, "Let's see it, but real slow. If you try anything funny, I'll shoot you in the cornea."

I lowered my hands super slo-mo and said, "It's in my pocket. May I reach into my jacket?"

She nodded, so I produced my school ID.

She took it, glanced at my name, and said, "Well, I'll be damned. You really are Leonard Peacock. What a stupid name."

I said, "Why are you crying?"

I saw her trigger finger twitch and I thought I was about to get maced, but instead she put my school ID into her purse and said, "Why are you following me, really? Did someone pay you? What do they want?"

"No. It's nothing like that at all."

She moved the Mace a few inches closer to my face, pointed at my left eye, and said, "Don't fuck with me, Leonard Peacock. Did Brian put you up to this? *Huh?* Tell me!"

I put my hands up again and said, "I don't know any Brian. I'm just a dumb kid. I dress up like an adult and skip school every once in a while to see what being an adult is like. Okay? I just want to know if growing up's worth it. That's all. And so I follow the most miserable-looking adult to work, because I just know that's going to be me someday—the most miserable adult on the train. I need to know if I can take it."

She said, "Take what?"

I said, "Being a miserable adult."

She lowered her Mace. "Really?"

I nodded.

She said, "You're absolutely crazy, aren't you?"

I nodded again.

"But not dangerous, right? You're a lamb."

I shook my head no, because I wasn't a threat back then. And then I nodded, because I wasn't a wolf or a lion or anything predatory at the time.

She said, "Okay. Do you drink coffee?"

ELEVEN

She took me to this coffee place close to the alley where she stole my school ID. It was mostly old people eating bagels and slurping joe.

She started talking about how stressed out she was and how there was this guy at her work named Brian whom she had screwed once and he was now using that against her because they were up for the same promotion. Her mother was dying in some hospice center in New Jersey, which was where she had spent the previous night. She had really wanted to stay with her mother because her mom was close to the end of her life, but this woman knew that—while no one would tell her she couldn't be there for her mother's passing—Brian would use her absence from work as a way to beat her out for the position.

Or at least that's what I understood.

She was rambling and slurring words like she was drunk and she kept waving her hands and she wouldn't take off her sunglasses even inside the coffee shop. She talked for an hour or so, and I was beginning to think she was a great big liar because if she left her dying mom to get ahead at work, why the hell would she waste her time with me at the coffee shop? Wouldn't Brian use missing work—for any reason at all—against her?

I was thinking about all of this when she said, "So what have you learned following around adults? Spying on us?"

I said, "I don't know."

"Don't lie to me. You owe me an explanation, Leonard Peacock."

And so I swallowed and said, "I'm not finished researching, which is why I followed you today."

"What have you learned today from me?"

"Truthfully?"

She nodded.

So I said, "You seem really unhappy. And most of the people I follow are the same. It seems like they don't like their jobs and yet they also don't like going home either. It's like they hate every aspect of their lives."

She laughed and said, "You need to follow people on the train to figure that out?"

And I said, "I was hoping that I had it wrong."

And she said, "Don't all the kids in your high school seem miserable too? I hated high school. *HATED it!*"

And I said, "Yeah, most of them do seem miserable. Although they try to fake it the best they can. Kids fake it better than adults, right? My theory is that we lose the ability to be happy as we age."

She smiled. "So if you've got it all figured out, why follow adults like me?"

"Like I said before, I was hoping that I'm wrong, that life gets better for some people when they get older, and even the most miserable people—such as you and me—might be able to enjoy at least some aspect of adulthood. Like those ads where gay guys talk about being picked on in high school but then they grew up and discovered that adult life is like heaven. They say it gets better. I want to believe that happiness might at least be possible later on in life for people prone to sadness."

She swatted my words out of the air with her hand and said, "All ads are lies. Life doesn't get better at all. Adulthood is hell. And everything I told you about myself was a lie too. I made everything up just to see who you were because I thought they paid you to be a spy. But the joke's on me because you really are just a crazy, sad, underfed high school student who follows random people. That's sick. Perverted. I'm keeping your ID and if I ever see you again I'm pressing charges and getting a restraining order."

She stood up and glared down at me through her huge sunglasses.

"This little prick follows women into dark alleys and asks them intimate questions. He's a true pervert. Do with him as you will," she said loudly to everyone eating breakfast, and then her heels clicked out of the shop—*POW! POW! POW! POW!*

I could tell everyone was still looking at me and so I shrugged and said, "Women!" too loudly. It was supposed to be a joke to break the tension, but it didn't work. Everyone[23] in the coffee shop was frowning.

I figured the woman was really deranged—I had simply picked a femme fatale to follow, there were surely better case studies to find, happier adults prone to sadness, and she was just an unlucky fluke—but the problem was that she sort of reminded me of Linda, who also thinks I'm a pervert.

And what the 1970s sunglasses woman had said was so mean, public, and maybe true, that I started to cry right there, which made me really *SEEM* like a pervert.

Not big boo-hoo tears.

I pretty much hid the fact that I was crying, but my lips trembled and my eyes got all moist before I could wipe them away with my sleeve.

"I'M NOT A FUCKING PERVERT!" I yelled at the people staring at me, although I'm not sure why.

The words just sort of shot out of my mouth.

I'M!
NOT!
A!
FUCKING!
PERVERT!

They all winced.

---

23 All adults.

A few people stuck money under their utensils and left, even though they weren't finished eating.

This huge muscle-inflated tattooed cook came out from the kitchen and said, "Why don't you just pay your bill and leave, kid? Okay?"

Just like always I could tell I was the problem—that the coffee shop would be better off once I was no longer around—so I pulled out my wallet and handed him all my money even though we only had a coffee each, and in a normal speaking voice, I said, "I'm not a pervert."

No one would make eye contact with me, not even the cook, who was looking at the money now, maybe to make sure it wasn't counterfeit, which is when I realized that the truth doesn't matter most of the time, and when people have awful ideas about your identity, that's just the way it will stay no matter what you do.

So I didn't wait for change.

I got the hell out of there.

I went to the park and watched the pigeons bob their heads and I felt so so lonely that I hoped someone would come along and stick a knife into my ribs just so they could have my empty wallet.

I imagined all of my blood flowing out into the snow and watching it turn a beautiful crimson color as Philadelphians walked by in a great big hurry, not even pausing to admire the beauty of red snow, let alone register the fact that a high school kid was dying right in front of their eyes.

The thought was comforting somehow and made me smile.

I also kept oscillating between wanting that crazy 1970s sunglasses woman's mom to die a horrible painful cringe-inducing death and wanting her mom to live and start to get healthier—younger even, like the two of them might even begin aging backward all the way to childhood—even though the femme fatale probably made the entire mother-dying story up just to mess with my head. But she had to have a mother who was either dead or elderly, and so it was nice to think of them getting younger together rather than older, regardless of whether they deserved it or not.

It was a confusing day, and I felt like I was in some Bogart black-and-white picture where women are crazy and men pay hefty emotional fees for getting involved with "the fairer sex," as Walt says.

I remember skipping four days of school after my encounter with the 1970s sunglasses woman just so Walt and I could watch good old Bogie keep things orderly in black-and-white Hollywood land.

My high school called a hundred million times before Linda checked the home answering machine[24] from NYC, and, to be fair, she actually had a driver bring her home that

_____
24 Answering machine in 2011? *What?* Sad but true. Linda doesn't like to give out her cell number to "non-industry people," like the office workers at my high school, because she thinks she's Donatella Versace.

night and stayed with me for a day or two, because I was really fucked up—not talking and just sort of really depressed—staring at walls and pushing the heels of my hands into my eyes until they felt like they would pop.

Any normal mom would have taken me to a therapist or at least a doctor, but not Linda. I heard her talking on the phone to her French boyfriend and she actually said, "I won't let some therapist blame me for Leo's problems." And that's when I really knew I was on my own—that I couldn't count on Linda to save me.

But somehow I pulled myself together.

I started talking again, went back to school, and an extremely relieved Linda left me alone once more.

Fashion called.

There were camisoles[25] with built-in bras to design, so I, of course, understood her need to float away to New York.

And life went on.

---

25 How does a teenage boy know the word *camisoles*? Three words: *Fashion designer mother.*

TWELVE

I walk into A.P. English halfway through the period and Mrs. Giavotella stares at me for just about seven minutes before she says, "How nice of you to join us, Mr. Peacock. See me after class."

My A.P. English teacher looks like a cannonball. She's short and round and has these stubby limbs that make me wonder if she can touch the top of her head. She never wears a dress or a skirt but is always in overstuffed pants that are about to explode and a huge blouse that hangs down almost to her knees, covering her belly. A beaded line of sweat perpetually sits just above her upper lip.

I nod and take my seat.

The troglodyte football player who doesn't even belong in A.P. but just so happens to sit directly behind me—that guy knocks my Bogart hat off my head and everyone sees my new fucked-up haircut before I can get my skull covered again.

"What the—?" this girl Kat Davis whispers, making me realize my hair looks worse than I had imagined.

Mrs. Giavotella gives me a look like she's really worried for me all of a sudden, and I look back at her like *please return to the lesson so everyone will stop looking at me because if you don't I will pull the P-38 from my backpack and start firing away.*

"Mr. Adams," Mrs. Giavotella says to the kid behind me. "If you were Dorian Gray—if there was a picture of you that changed according to your behavior, how would that picture look right about now?"

"I didn't knock Leonard's hat off, if that's what you're implying. He knocked it off himself. I saw him do it. I didn't do anything wrong."

Mrs. Giavotella looks at him for a second, and I can tell she believes him. Then she looks at me, like she's wondering if I really did knock my own hat off, so I say, "Why would I knock my own hat off? What purpose would that serve?"

"Why would you interrupt my lesson by arriving late?" she says, and then gives me this lame look that's supposed to intimidate and control me—and it probably would on any other day. But I have the P-38 in my backpack, and therefore am uncontrollable.

Mrs. Giavotella says, "So. Back to Mr. Dorian Gray."

I don't really listen to the class discussion, which is all about a painting that gets uglier and uglier as its subject ages and becomes more and more corrupt, but magically never ages himself at all. It sounds like an interesting book, and I probably would have read it if I weren't so obsessed with reading *Hamlet* over and over again. If I weren't going to shoot Asher Beal and kill myself this afternoon, I'd probably read *The Picture of Dorian Gray* next. I've liked everything we've read in Mrs. Giavotella's class this year, even though she's always going on and on about the bullshit A.P. exam and dangling the college-credit carrot way more than she should. It's almost obscene.

Mostly, as I'm sitting here in A.P. English, I think about the way my classmates are always raising their hands and sucking up to Mrs. Giavotella just so she will give them As, which they will send to Harvard or Princeton or Stanford or where-fucking-ever, to go along with their lies about how much community service they supposedly did and essays about how much they care about poor minority children they'll never meet in real life or how they are going to save the world armed with nothing but a big heart and an Ivy League education.

"Save the world in your college application essays," Mrs. Giavotella likes to say.

If my classmates put as much effort into making our community better as they give to the college-application process, this place would be a utopia.

Appearances, appearances.

The great façade.

How to Live Blindly in a Blind World 101.

So much bullshit gets flung around in here, the stench

gets so strong that you can hardly breathe. The best thing about killing myself will be that I'll never have to go to a fake university and wear one of those standard college sweatshirts that's supposed to prove I'm smart or something. I'm pretty proud of the fact that I will die without officially taking the SATs. Even though Linda and everyone here at my high school has begged me to take that stupid test just because I did so well on the practice one a few years ago.

Illogical.

Epic fail.

Somehow the class ends and I remember I'm supposed to speak with Mrs. Giavotella, so I just stay put when everyone scrambles out the door.

She walks over all slow and dramatic, sits on the desk in front of me so that her feet are resting on the seat, her knees clamped together tight so that I don't get a direct view of her overly taxed zipper, which I appreciate very much, and says, "So, do you want to talk about what happened to your hair?"

"No, thank you."

"You sure?"

"Yes."

"Okay, then. Why exactly were you late for my class?"

"I don't know."

"Not good enough."

"I'm thinking of dropping down to the honors track. You won't have to worry about me then."

"Not a chance."

I'm not really sure what she wants from me, so I look out the window at the few leaves clinging to the small Japanese maple outside.

She says, "I graded your *Hamlet* exam. How do you think you did?"

I shrug.

"Your essay was very interesting."

I keep looking at the few clinging leaves that seem to shiver whenever the wind blows.

"Of course, you completely ignored the prompt."

"You asked the wrong question," I say.

"I beg your pardon?"

"No offense, but I think you asked the wrong essay question."

She forces an incredulous laugh and says, "So you gave me the right question."

"Yes."

"Which was?"

"You read my essay, right?"

"Do you really think Shakespeare is trying to justify suicide—that the entire play is an argument for self-slaughter?"

"Yes."

"But Hamlet doesn't commit suicide."

"You *did* read my essay, right?"

Mrs. Giavotella smoothes out her pant legs, rubbing her palms down her thighs, and then says, "I noticed you didn't bring your copy of the text to the open-book test. And yet you quoted extensively. Do you really have so many quotes memorized? Is that possible?"

I shrug, because why does that even matter? It's like my English teacher gets off on having supposedly smart people in her class, and yet she doesn't even realize what's important about the books and plays we read. She doesn't understand what's important about me either.

"Your essay was brilliant, Leonard. Perhaps the finest I've come across in all of my nineteen years of teaching. I read it several times. You have a real way with words. And your arguments—you could be a fantastic lawyer if you wanted to be."

I keep staring at those few clinging leaves, waiting for her to flip the praise into scorn like she always does.

Who the fuck would want to be a lawyer? Being forced to argue for money—supporting sides you don't even believe in.

After a dramatic pause, she says, "But you didn't answer any of the simple multiple-choice questions. Why?"

"You only ask those to make sure everyone read the play," I say. "My essay clearly proves that I read the play, right? I demonstrated proficiency, did I not?"

"They were worth thirty points. You didn't demonstrate the ability to follow simple directions. That counts in my class, and in life too. No matter how smart you may be, you're going to have to follow instructions once you leave this high school."

I laugh because we're talking about her grades and points

as if they're real or something. And knowing that I'm about to kill Asher Beal and then myself makes this conversation all the more absurd and irrelevant.

"I don't really care about the grade. You can fail me. It doesn't matter."

"That's very noble of you, but you have to think about your future, Leonard."

"Do you think Hamlet would have followed directions if he had taken this exam? Do you?"

"That's hardly the point."

"Then why do you make us study characters like Hamlet—heroes—if we're not supposed to act like them? If we're supposed to worry about points and college-acceptance letters and all the rest. Do what everyone else is doing."

"Hamlet went to college," she says weakly, because she knows I'm right. She knows she's fighting on the wrong side.

I smile and keep looking at the tree. She has no clue. Never in her wildest dreams would she imagine I have a Nazi gun on me. Her imagination is so limited. She has a multiple-choice-question-making imagination. It makes me laugh, how stupid our A.P. English teacher is.

She says, "I've tried to contact your—"

I use my acting voice to say, "Make you a wholesome answer. My wit's diseased. But, sir, such answer as I can make, you shall command—or, rather, as you say, *my mother*. Therefore no more but to the matter. My mother, you say—"

Mrs. Giavotella just sort of stares at me like she's afraid, so

I say, "You're supposed to jump in as Rosencrantz," and in my acting voice I say, " 'Then thus she says: your behavior hath struck her into amazement and admiration.' You see—I was quoting from *Hamlet*. You did realize that, right? You can't be that much of a shitty teacher. *Come on!*"

Her face goes blank and her mouth becomes an O, like I slapped her hard.

Eventually, she stands and walks to her desk.

I watch her write a pass.

She hands it to me and in this new stern faraway detached voice she says, "I'm here to help, Leonard. I'm glad that you found *Hamlet* so stimulating. I won't pretend to know what's going on with you, but I have to report your bizarre behavior to Guidance. I just want you to know that. And I'm not really sure what you're after, but I try very hard to be a good teacher. I spend a lot of time and energy on my tests and lesson plans. I care about all of my students, thank you very much." In a whisper, she says, *"If you want to throw that in my face then— then you can go to hell."* Much louder she says, "When you're willing to talk straight with me, I'm willing to listen. But if you ever come to my class again even one second late, you won't be permitted entrance. *You understand me?"*

I look into Mrs. Giavotella's eyes and her lids are quivering, which is when I realize that she's going to cry just as soon as I leave the room. And this is going to be her last memory of me. I'm not really sure why, but I feel terrible all of a sudden. Like I want to pull out the P-38 and off myself in the bathroom stall. If I didn't have to deliver the other three presents and shoot Asher Beal in the face, I probably would just get it over with and be done with everything.

I have the pass in my hand and now Mrs. Giavotella's looking at the almost completely bare Japanese maple outside her classroom window.

What makes sad people want to look at that tree?

Her back fat is hanging over her bra strap and it makes me wonder if she was picked on a lot in high school for being so short, overweight, and squishy. She probably was, which makes me feel even worse.

"You're a good teacher," I say. "I knocked my own hat off too. I'm an asshole, okay? A HUGE asshole. I don't deserve to have such a fine teacher as yourself. *Okay?* Don't worry about the stupid things I said. I'm sorry I interrupted your class today. My head's not right. I'll answer multiple-choice questions in the future if it will make you happy. I know you work hard on your lesson plans and—"

Without facing me she says, "Just go, Leonard. *Please.*"

"Are you okay?"

"*I'd like you to leave now*," she says in a shaky voice.

So I do.

THIRTEEN
LETTER FROM THE FUTURE NUMBER 2

My Dearest Hamlet,

I'm five foot five with short brown hair (think pixie cut), a cute ass (or so you say, and I believe you because you can't keep your hands off it!), and I wear a full (perky) B-cup. You find me irresistible and we make love at least once a day, but usually manage to do it multiple times employing all sorts of creative positions too. That ought to get your horny little teenage mind reeling.

Can you even imagine sex every day with another human being?

You told me that when you were a teenager you believed you wouldn't ever have consensual sex with anyone—that you would die a consensual virgin, which would have been a shame, because let me tell you something, you LOVE sex.

Sometimes I make you beg, and beg you do.

And if you would just ask a girl on a date, Mr. King of Masturbation, you would definitely be surprised, and maybe we'd have fewer issues to work through when we first get together. Not that I want you fooling around with little chicken-assed high school girls before we meet! Ha!

You get to make love to me in the future hundreds (thousands?) of times!

Doesn't that make you want to live on into adulthood?

Aren't I enough?

All joking aside—for a couple that lives with a small child and an old man in a lighthouse, our sex life is mind-blowing.

We work all day outside, doing routine rounds, excavating buildings, checking our flotation devices, testing the radioactive levels of the water, and then we swim for hours and hours, so our bodies are firm and tan and beautiful, unlike the fat mush they would have turned into had we gone to the enclosed cities and worked desk jobs where no one ever sees the sun.

We are very, very lucky.

In many ways, we avoided adulthood.

Outpost 37 is our own private utopia.

You call it "second childhood."

Do you want to know how we meet?

Should I ruin the surprise?

I feel like I better entice you. It would be a shame if you never made it this far—to the best part of your life.

After the war, when things settled and the North American Land Collective was formed, thousands of nomads were forced to repatriate through camps set up along the new controlled borders, which began in the state you now call Ohio, but have since been forced much farther west due to rising water, earthquakes, and general instability. Those who repatriated were absorbed by one of the many enclosed cities that were built and continue to be built upward. Those who refused to repatriate were considered a threat to the new order and therefore were hunted and, once captured, given the choice between death and forced labor in outdoor prison camps.

From what you've told me, the bounty hunters employed by the Repatriate Act of 2023 caught you asleep in a cave. You were surviving off wild berries and the small rodents you could kill, mostly rats. It was not a good life for you, I'm afraid, and you were not very well mentally. Actually, you were certifiably insane.

You did a tour overseas, during the Great War of 2018. You won't talk about your time in the military, but sometimes you have nightmares when you scream about killing. Again, you won't talk about it so I don't know more.

You say, "That was the before life. Let's live in the now life."

And since you are generally happy when you are awake and are such a good husband, I don't push it with the questions about the past and the night terrors.

But back to the story of how we met. You were brought into an outdoor labor camp, and you refused to work or talk, even when they withheld food and water and finally tortured you, almost to death.

When they decided that you were expendable and that it had been a mistake to bring you in alive, you were saved by a request from the heartland for test subjects and shipped to a government testing facility. I just so happened to be an administrative operator back then, and you were assigned to me.

I was a scientist working on a drug that made it easier for adults to conform to the new enclosed world. The idea was to rid the planet of rebellious people and to make sure we curbed the human tendency to disagree and argue, which has led us to nuclear war and all that followed.

Mother Earth was angry with us, and so we had to "teach ourselves to be better children," which was the tagline the new North American Land Collective government preached.

At first you wouldn't speak to me either. I had you in a padded cell and I would talk to you via speakers. But you just sat in the corner with your head between your knees, getting skinnier and skinnier.

At night we'd gas you, and then my aides would give you shots full of vitamins, nutrients, and the experimental chemicals.

I don't remember why I decided to read to you, but we started with Shakespeare—*Hamlet*—which was damn lucky for us. Made me believe in fate again, if you'll allow me to be mystical.

I read, saying, "Act I. Scene I. Elsinore. A platform before the Castle. Francisco at his post. Enter to him Bernardo. *Who's there?*"

That's when you lifted your head and said, "Nay, answer me: stand, and unfold yourself."

I was shocked. You hadn't spoken once and here you were reciting the next line in *Hamlet*. It was like I found the key to your mouth. So I read on, saying, "Long live the king!"

"Bernardo?" you said.

"He," I replied.

"You come most carefully upon your hour," you said, and then we traded lines from *Hamlet* all day long.

A few times I tried to break and ask you questions, but you would only say, "More words! Words, words, words!"

And for a week or so we played this game—putting on the play, just the two of us through speakers.

You were so passionate about it, such a good actor, actually—reciting Hamlet's soliloquies with such zeal and conviction that I began to think you were perhaps once a budding movie star.

Eventually, I broke protocol and entered the padded cell so that we might read the play together in person. That's how taken I was with your ability to breathe life into Shakespeare's lines.

We acted out *Hamlet* for weeks, and the drugs we gave you started to work—you lost the wild look in your eyes and eventually began to speak to me like a regular human being. Only you weren't regular at all—you were full of magic.

I remember the first thing you said too, when you finally broke character. You said, "Can I take you to dinner sometime?"

It was a ridiculous thing to say, since you were locked up.

But I laughed, and you smiled.

You began to tell me the story of your life, and I broke protocol again by telling you mine.

I began to take you out into the world—partly to show my superiors how I had tamed the wild man with my science, reclaimed his mind for the good of society, but mostly because I was in love with you.

As you will learn, my father was a high-ranking military man during the Great War and many of the North American Land Collective leaders owe him favors. It wasn't really all that hard to get both of us transferred to Outpost 37 under his command.

Once the paperwork was complete, after I had finished my drug study and vitamin Z was introduced successfully into the controlled population, we were flown by helicopter to Outpost 37.

My father threw open his arms and said, "Welcome home."

You and Dad took to each other right away, and he presided over our wedding a few weeks later when we discovered that I was pregnant.

That's right, Leonard. You'll be hearing from our daughter next. You love S even more than you love me, and I don't mind that one bit, because I love you both to death.

You are a fantastic dad.

Fantastic!

And I know that your childhood wasn't all that great—that you felt a lot of pain, and that you are in a lot of pain right now. But maybe you have to go through all that so you'll learn just how important having a happy childhood can be, so you will provide one for our daughter.

I wish I could send you a video or a picture of you and S playing in the water with Horatio the dolphin. If you could see that, you'd know that all of the pain you have to endure to get here, where you are happy in the future, is most definitely worth it.

Even though she's getting too old to be sleeping with us, she still falls asleep with her head on your chest every night. You kiss the top of her hair before you man the lighthouse with Dad and me.

We send out the beam for twenty minutes, and then conserve energy for twenty minutes, repeating the forty-minute cycle all night long. Three or so minutes before we switch the light back on, after our eyes have just begun to adjust to the dark, you and I always go out onto the observation deck to search for shooting stars. There are a lot these days and we've been keeping track of who spots the most. This year I'm beating you 934 to 812. We're hoping to get to 1,000 each before the year ends, and it's looking good.

And we kiss every time we spot a shooting star too.

So we've kissed 1,746 times on the observation deck this year alone, and many more times have we kissed elsewhere.

I like that you are so affectionate with me. You always say you're making up for lost time and that

you wished we could have met earlier in life, so that
we would have been able to spend more time together.

It's a good life, Leonard.

Hold on.

The future is better.

We have so much sex!

Your daughter is beautiful.

And my dad becomes a dad to you too—just like
you always wanted.

Just hold on, okay?

Please.

Love,
Don't-You-Dare-Call-Me-Ophelia,
A

FOURTEEN

My friend Baback is of Iranian descent, but when I first met him, he used to tell everyone he was Persian, because most American teenagers don't know that Iran used to be Persia, and most American teens have watched enough news to hate Iran.

Back when he was a freshman, if you gave Baback some wrinkles and a salt-and-pepper beard he'd look exactly like the current Iranian president, Mahmoud Ahmadinejad, which could cause him problems, especially during patriotic times like 9/11 anniversaries, and whenever Ahmadinejad made anti-Semitic, anti-Israel, and anti-American comments, which was all the time.

At the very least you would have thought that Baback definitely could be related to Ahmadinejad, that's how much he used to look like the Iranian president.

I met Baback during freshmen orientation, right after he came to America and ended up in our school. For a year I saw him around the halls looking tiny and terrified, dressed in really formal clothes—like if you gave him a tie, he'd be a prep school kid in a uniform. He had a backpack that was bigger than him, and he was always carrying this violin case—like everywhere he went. He wouldn't leave it in a locker, except during gym class, when he was forced to—I know because we had gym together as sophomores.

There was this one gym class where we were playing floor hockey and our teacher Mr. Austin got called away on some sort of business for ten minutes. Baback and I were on the same team and not really participating all that much. We were sort of just standing in the middle of the gym holding sticks, watching everyone else chase and slap at a little orange ball.

Asher Beal was on the other team, and just as soon as he saw that Mr. Austin was no longer in the gym, he slap-shot the ball at Baback. It hit him right between the eyes. Baback blinked a few times in this really comical way, which made everyone else laugh, but I could tell that Baback was actually hurt so I didn't laugh. I remember feeling hot, like my face was on fire, because I already wanted to kill Asher Beal back then, but I still thought I might want a future so I wasn't really actively planning his execution, well not consciously anyway.

I saw all of the stupid übermorons with whom Asher now hangs exchange glances and then they all started to smile in this really creepy way. It was almost like they were a flock of evil birds or a school of evil fish, because they all instinctively reacted in unison without even talking.

Do übermorons excrete pheromones?

Everyone started to pass to Baback, and just as soon as his stick touched the ball, Asher or one of his übermoron cronies cross-checked Baback so hard he became airborne. Baback tried to flick away the orange ball really quickly, as if that could protect him, but they kept checking him whether he had the ball or not. He was getting killed, and I wanted to tell him to stay down or run up into the stands, but it was like he didn't want to believe that he was being targeted for violence. It's like he had to believe we were all better than that here in America. Maybe because that's what his parents told him when he left Iran—America is better.

Several people checked Baback before Asher lined up a shot that sent the little Iranian kid flying into the stands. His feet went up above his head and I heard his skull thump the wooden bleacher slat.

Almost everyone[26] was laughing really hard, because Baback's body spun around like a windmill and now his feet were in the air, his torso stuck in the bleachers.

But Baback didn't get up this time.

---

26 There were a few kids who looked just as sickened as I was by the übermorons' behavior but they didn't let Asher see their disgust. No one wanted to be the next target, and that's just how übermorons like it—the secret to their power.

"Come on," Asher said to Baback, like they were friends. "You're okay."

Asher sort of pulled Baback out of the stands and you could tell Baback was woozy because he was swaying like a field of wheat in a beer commercial.

"Welcome to America," Asher said—even though Baback had been in our school for more than a year—and then Asher patted Baback on the back twice.

Whenever I replay this memory, I see myself running, and before I know it I've left my feet and I'm a flying cross-check. In my mind, my hockey stick turns into a samurai sword and I decapitate Asher with an awesome swipe so that his head flies through the air and right through the basketball net.

Two points!

But in real life, I just stood there.

In the locker room they started in on Baback again while he was changing.

"What's this?" Asher asked as he plucked the violin case from Baback's locker.

Baback was trying to get his pants on and actually fell over. His little naked brown chest was concave. His nipples were purple-black. "That's my grandfather's violin. Careful. *Please*. It's been in my family for generations!" Baback's eyes were wide open—he looked terrified.

No one was really paying me any attention, so I snuck up behind Asher and snatched the violin out of his hands before he realized what was going on.

"Peacock?" Asher said.

I gave the violin back to Baback, and he clutched it to his chest like it was a baby.

"You touch him or his violin again and I tell everyone the secret," I said. The words just came out of my mouth before I could think. Suddenly my heart was pounding and my tongue was bone dry. But I added, "I swear to god. I'll tell everyone. Everyone!"

Asher's eyes got really small because he knew exactly what I was referring to, but he said, "I have no idea what you're talking about, Peacock. You're so fucking weird."

Asher laughed and then turned away from Baback and me.

I could tell that some of Asher's friends were like— *What secret?*—and that was my power over Asher Beal back then.

He backed down from me, and that cost him.

Baback just got changed and left the locker room without even thanking me or anything, which depressed me a little, truth be told.

Just to make sure he was okay, I looked for Baback next period at lunch, but he wasn't there, which was strange because all sophomores had the same cafeteria time.

The next day in gym I watched to make sure Asher and his übermoron cronies left Baback alone, and they did. So halfway through gym class, as we both pretended to play floor hockey, I jogged up to Baback and said, "Why weren't you in lunch yesterday? Did you go to the nurse?"

"I don't want any trouble," Baback said without looking at me. His eyes followed the little orange ball that the rest of our gym class was running after and slapping at. "Just leave me alone."

No one messed with Baback in the locker room either, which made me feel a little proud.

I decided to follow Baback when the period was over and I watched him meet the janitor at the auditorium. The janitor let Baback in and then left. The auditorium is in a part of the school that isn't used for much else, so there's usually no one around there. I looked through the window in the door and watched Baback take his violin out of the case, tune, and then begin to practice.

To say he was amazing would be an understatement.

He was world-class at fifteen—better than anyone you will ever hear play the violin.

A musical wizard.

I watched through the glass and listened to that little tiny boy make gigantic swirls of rising and falling notes that made my chest ache and ache.

It was so beautiful.

The best part was that he closed his eyes and kept nodding to the rhythm of his bow sawing, and you could tell that when he played his violin, he wasn't a tiny misplaced Iranian boy living in a secretly racist town—no, he was a god in complete control of his world.

It was like the violin bow was a magic wand, and the

vibrations that came out of the holes cut into that little wooden instrument were a force that few could reckon with.

He seemed to grow tall in front of me.

And I understood why he didn't need friends or to be accepted at our shitty racist high school, because he had his music, and that was so much better than anything we had to offer.

"You're a genius," I said when he exited the auditorium.

Baback just blinked the same way he did when he'd been struck between the eyes with the orange hockey ball. "Were you spying on me?"

"How did you learn to play like that?"

"I don't want any trouble," he said, and then walked away.

The next day I made sure to be there when the janitor let Baback in.

Baback said, "I need to practice."

"I just want to listen. I'll sit in the back and won't interrupt."

Baback sighed, took the stage, and began to play.

I sat in the last row, closed my eyes, and was transported out of our terrible high school and into a new, better place.

When the music stopped, I opened my eyes and across the tops of so many rows of seats, I yelled, "Did you write that music?"

He blinked again and yelled back, "It's Paganini. The violin concertos. Bits of the solos that I can't get right—*ever*."

"They were perfect! I love it. This is the greatest secret.

Something miraculous happens every day at this high school, and I'm the only student who knows about it."

"Don't tell anyone, please!" Baback yelled back. "About my using the auditorium. I'm not supposed to let anyone know. My parents had to beg for permission. If other students ask to use the auditorium, I won't be allowed to practice in here alone anymore. *Please!*"

I could tell that he was really worried about this, so I walked down the aisle and when I reached him I said, "Let me listen and I won't tell a soul. I promise. Nor will I ever interrupt you. I'd never want to alter what happens here. Never. Think of me like a ghost."

He nodded reluctantly.

And for the rest of the school year, I listened to him play.

It was kind of weird, because we never talked.

He didn't seem interested in me at all.

I could tell he didn't really want to be my friend—that he just wanted to be left alone with his music, and I respected that.

I mostly wanted to be left alone too—so we shared a large space and were alone together, if that makes any sense at all.

But on the last day of our sophomore year, I broke protocol, gave Baback a standing ovation, and yelled, "Bravo!" when he finished playing.

He smiled, but didn't say anything.

"Until we meet again, maestro!" I yelled down over a sea of empty red seats, and then left.

When we began our junior year, Baback was changed.

He returned five inches taller and was ripped with so many bulging muscles. He'd grown out his thick black hair and began keeping it in a ponytail. And he had these fantastic cheekbones that all of the girls noticed. He no longer looked like a kid to pick on or pity.

When I went to the auditorium during lunch period, he broke the silence by saying, "I've been thinking about you, Leonard. Why do you come here every day to hear me play?"

"It's the best thing that happens at this school on a daily basis. I wouldn't miss it."

"You should pay to listen," he said. "I'm providing a service for you. Artists need to be compensated. If you give it away for free, people stop appreciating art. It loses its value."

"What happened to you?"

"What do you mean?"

"You look different. You talk now. You seem confident."

He laughed and said, "I spent the summer in Iran studying music. I grew up a little, I guess. Literally and metaphorically. But you're either paying for the privilege of listening to me play, or you're going to leave."

"How much do you want?"

"I don't know," he said in a way that suggested he was expecting me to leave. "Maybe pay what you will? *But something*. I'm not playing for free anymore."

"Why don't you leave your violin case open and I'll put

something in it every day I come listen? I've seen musicians do that on the streets of Philly."

"Okay," he said, and then began to play.

When he was finished, I walked up to the stage and dropped a five-dollar bill into his violin case. He nodded, which I assumed meant he was okay with the amount.

So I gave him my lunch money every day for the rest of the year—except for a few times when either he or I was absent, or when the drama club was in the auditorium creating sets for plays and Baback didn't practice.

My daily donations added up to more than eight hundred dollars by the end of the year. I know because Baback told me the exact number on the last day of classes junior year, saying, "I sent every penny to True Democracy in Iran, a nonprofit fighting for, well, *true democracy in Iran*."

I thought it was a good cause to support, so I nodded.

I saw Baback in the hallway during finals and when I flagged him down, before I could explain what I wanted, he said, "Do you want to hang out sometime, Leonard? Maybe see a movie or something? We don't really know each other, do we? It's kind of odd, don't you think?"

I thought about it and said, "I hope you won't take this the wrong way, but listening to you play your violin is by far the best part of my day. And I think part of the magic is that I don't really know you at all, but only as a performing musician. And I worry that if I got to know you as a friend or whatever, your music might not seem as magical. *Did that ever happen to you?* You think someone is really important and different, but then you get to know them and it ruins everything? *Do you know what I'm talking about?*"

He laughed and said, "No. Not really."

"Can I listen to you practice sometime over the summer? I'll pay you five dollars."

"Well, I'm not sure that's a great idea. It would probably weird out my parents if you were just sitting in my practice space staring at me. And I'm going to Iran at the end of the month to visit relatives and continue my musical training with my grandfather. So I won't be around much," he said, obviously backpedaling, maybe because he found my explanation weird.

"Okay, then. See you next year," I said, and handed him an envelope I had labeled TRUE DEMOCRACY IN IRAN!

I had talked Linda into donating five hundred bucks as a tax write-off. She needs those for her business and is always eager to buy me off/assuage her guilty absent-mom conscience with money. The check was inside, but I didn't want him to open it in front of me, so I said, "That's for later. I look forward to listening next year. Enjoy your time abroad."

This year when I met him at the auditorium during senior lunch he was even taller and more confident-looking. Baback smiled and said, "I told my grandmother about you and your donation. She made you some tasbih beads. Persian prayer beads. But some people use them as worry beads. Here."

He handed me this long looped string of reddish-brown wooden beads with a tassel on the end.

"Thanks," I said, and put the beads around my neck.

He smiled and then said, "You don't have to pay to listen to my music anymore. You can listen for free. My grandfather says that music is a gift you give to others when you can. I told him about you and the donations. He said I should play for you without charging money. So I will."

I nodded and took my regular seat at the back of the auditorium.

Baback played his music.

I didn't think it was possible, but he was better—more magical—than the year before.

I closed my eyes, listened, and disappeared.

FIFTEEN

Baback's playing is one of the few things around here that actually make me feel better, and since I've already made up my mind to shoot Asher Beal and off myself, I don't want to risk listening to Baback work his violin. I'm afraid his music might seduce me, trick me into living for another day—like it has so many times before. So when I enter the auditorium, I say, "Baback, I won't be listening to you play today."

"What?" he says with a mock-horrified face. He's wearing dark jeans, checkered Vans, and a Harold & Kumar T-shirt—and I think about how much he's changed, been Americanized, even if he's still unlike the other students here. "And just why are you breaking tradition, may I ask?"

Instead of answering his question, I pull out his present from my backpack—an envelope wrapped in pink paper—and I say, "This is for you." My voice booms and echoes in the huge, empty auditorium.

He looks me in the eye and says, "What is it?"

"I just want you to know that I really, really enjoy listening to you play your violin and that the lunch periods I spend lost in your music—well, let's just say you have no idea how much your violin music has saved me over the past few years. So many days I wouldn't make it if I didn't hear you play. You're a really gifted musician. I hope you'll never stop playing. I want to give you something to express my gratitude—to let you know that I value your playing more than you realize. It may just look like I'm sitting in the back of the room sleeping, but it's so much more than that—your music gives me something to look forward to each day—and it's like a friend to me. Maybe my best friend here at our high school. I just want to say thank you."

I can feel my eyes welling up, so I look down at my feet and extend the pink rectangle toward Baback.

He takes the envelope and says, "Why are you telling me this *today*, Leonard?"

"I just needed to give this to you. It's a present."

"Why's it wrapped in pink?"

"The color isn't really significant."

"Am I not getting something here?" he asks.

I sort of hope he'll figure out it's my birthday, but I'm not sure why. Still, I get excited thinking that he might guess it.

He peels off the wrapping paper, opens the envelope, reads the check I wrote out to True Democracy in Iran, and says, "Is this some sort of joke?"

"*What*? No. It's a check to help aid the freedom fighters in your country."

"You really expect me to believe this is real?"

"It's my college fund. I'm not going to college. I didn't even take the SAT."

"Why are you messing around like this? Do you even know what it's like for people living in Iran? This isn't a joke, Leonard. Some things you can't joke around about."

"I know. That check is real. I swear to god. Send it to the cause. You'll see. I hope the money helps the struggle. It's my entire college fund. My grandparents left me a ton of cash."

"What's wrong with you?"

"I thought you'd be happy."

He sighs and runs his hands through his hair, which is hanging freely to his shoulders today.

"Listen, I appreciate your sticking up for me when we were sophomores and I appreciate your...*support*. I get that you're a little off. That you march to your own drummer or whatever. I'm okay with that. But I've never done anything to you—never been mean at all—and yet you walk in here and insult me with this fake *six-figure* check. My grandparents have endured innumerable...you have no idea how hard it was for my family and...*you know what*," he says while putting his violin away, "I don't think I'm going to play today. And I don't think I want you listening to me anymore. Your being in the back of the auditorium—just sitting there every day—it's really starting to creep me out."

"The check's real," I say.

"Okay, Leonard."

"I'm fucking serious. That check is real! You're being an asshole. Go to the bank right now and you'll see what an asshole you're being."

"Why are you wearing that hat?" he says. "Did you cut off your hair?"

I look at him and can tell he doesn't really like me.

I was right; just as soon as you take the first step toward getting to know someone your own age, everything you thought was magical about that person turns to shit right in front of your face.

He's looking at me like he loathes me—like my face disgusts him—and I just want him to stop.

"Maybe you should talk to someone," he says. "Like Guidance."

"I tried talking to you and look where that got us."

"Listen, you obviously have problems, Leonard. I'm sorry for that. I really am. But there are people with worse problems than yours, I can assure you this. Leave this town once in a while and you'll see that I'm right. First-world problems. That's what you have."

He strides through the doors and I realize I must have really pissed him off, because it's the first time he hasn't practiced when the auditorium was available during lunchtime. The first time in three school years.

I pick up the check he left behind, sit down in one of those old-ass creaky seats, and ponder what he said about there being people with worse problems than mine. It takes me all of three seconds to conclude that's such a bullshit thing to say. Like the people in Iran are more important than me because their suffering is supposedly more acute.

Bullshit.

I like thinking all alone in the auditorium even when there is no violin music.

Maybe I never even needed Baback to begin with.

Maybe he's just like all the rest.

It's better here when I'm by myself.

Safer.

How do you measure suffering?

I mean, the fact that I live in a democratic country doesn't guarantee my life will be problem-free.

Far from it.

I understand that I am relatively privileged from a socio-economical viewpoint, but so was Hamlet—so are a lot of miserable people.

I bet there are people in Iran who are happier than I am—who wish to keep living there regardless of who is in charge politically, while I'm miserable here in this supposedly free country and just want out of this life at any cost.

I wonder if Baback will regret demeaning my suffering when he turns on the news tonight.

I kinda hope he'll feel responsible somehow—that it will make him so regretful he gets sick.

SIXTEEN

I see Asher Beal in the hallway. I make my hand into the shape of a gun and fire at him as he passes.

I miss twice, but then score a head shot.

"Dead!"

"What's wrong with you?" he says, shaking his soon-to-be leaky skull.

"Everything!" I yell. "Nothing! You choose!"

People in the hallway are looking at me like I'm crazy— like they wish I would disappear.

Asher Beal just walks away.

"I know where you live!" I yell at him.

Knowing that this will all end tonight, that I will cease to be—that makes this day so much easier. It's like I'm in a dream, floating through some ethereal world.[27]

---

27 Untethered from my awful future.

Two presents left to deliver, and then I can open the P-38 and go out on the same day I came in.

Happy birthday to me!

God, I can't wait.

"Leonard?" Mrs. Shanahan says.

My guidance counselor is wearing a lemon-yellow dress and has her red hair up in a bun today. She has these sky-blue glasses that dangle from her neck on a silver chain in a crazy ironic way, because she is way too young to wear her glasses on a chain. I wonder how she dresses when she's not in school and I see her as an after-hours punk rocker maybe. She's younger than most faculty members—Herr Silverman's age, probably.

"I'm hearing reports that you've been acting strangely today. Is that true?" she says to me right in the hallway as tons of kids pass by.

"What? I'm always strange, right? But I'm fine otherwise," I say, mostly because I don't want to miss Herr Silverman's Holocaust class, which is where I'm headed now.

I usually don't mind going to Mrs. Shanahan's office because she keeps a jar of lollipops on her desk and I always enjoy a root beer sucker midday, but I have to say good-bye to Herr Silverman before I exit the planet, and I don't want to miss his class. It's the one class I actually like. So I decide to put on a show for her.

"What's going on under that hat?" she asks.

"Just a haircut."

"Mrs. Giavotella said—"

"I'm not a very good barber, I'm afraid," I say, smiling and looking into her eyes all Hollywood. I'm a convincing actor when I need to be. "I'd show you my new look right now, but I'm a little self-conscious about it, hence the hat. Can I swing by eighth period? Would be happy to show you then and talk about whatever you'd like."

She looks into my eyes for a long time, like she's trying to tell whether I'm bullshitting her.

Deep down she absolutely knows I'm bullshitting her, I'm sure of it. But she has a million problems to solve, hundreds of students who need her help, endless asshole parents to deal with, mountains of paperwork, meetings in that awful room with the round table and the window air-conditioning unit they run even in winter because the meeting room is directly over the tropically hot boiler room, and so she knows the easiest thing to do is believe me.

She's fulfilled her obligation, assuaged her conscience by finding me in the hallway and giving me the chance to freak out, and I've played my role too, by remaining calm, pretending to be okay, and therefore giving her permission to cross me off her things-to-do list. Now she can move on, and I can too.

Once you understand how adults are controlled by the system, manipulating them is elementary.

"I've put aside a few root beer lollipops for you, because I was getting low," she says, and then smiles back at me.

If only you could solve all of your problems with candy, I think, *Mrs. Shanahan would be relevant.*

"We'll talk eighth period, right? Promise you'll come see me. I always look forward to a visit from Leonard Peacock."

She says that last bit almost like she's flirting with me, like we're going to have sex in her office if I show up. A lot of female teachers do this—flirt with male students. I wonder if that's the only way they know how to interact with men. Like they use their sexuality to get what they want. And I have to admit it works, because I really want to go see Mrs. Shanahan now, and if I hadn't already decided to kill myself, I would most certainly go to her office later—if only to collect my root beer lollipop and fantasize.

"Absolutely," I lie. "I will definitely come see my favorite, most beauteous and astute guidance counselor later this afternoon."

She sort of blushes and then smiles at me all pleased with herself.

When she turns, I say, "Mrs. Shanahan?" because I can't help myself.

"Yes, Leonard," she says, and spins around all Marilyn Monroe—her dress even flares out and rises a little.

"Thanks for checking up on me. You're a good counselor. One of the best."

"You're welcome," she says, and then lights up like the sun at noon, because she doesn't understand what I'm really saying.

She's just a high school guidance counselor after all. She can tell you what grade point average you need to get into Penn, but expecting more than that is pushing it. I was lucky to receive so many lollipops.

Just before she goes, almost as if she wants to acknowledge the fact that we're playing a game here—one with rules—she adds, "You *will* come visit me eighth period, right?"

"You know it," I lie.

I think about how she probably has my birthday written down in a file somewhere, but she deals with so many kids that I can't really be mad at her for forgetting.

In elementary school the teachers always remembered your birthday, and that was nicer. There were cupcakes or brownies, or at least cookies, and everyone sang in a way that made you feel really special and a part of something, even if you really hated all of your classmates deep down. There's a reason the elementary teachers did that. It wasn't just for fun. It was important.

And I wonder at what age it's appropriate to stop keeping track of everyone's birthday. When do we stop needing the people around us to acknowledge the fact that we are aging and changing and getting closer to our deaths? No one tells you this. It's like everyone remembers your birthday every single year and then suddenly you can't remember the last time someone sang the birthday song to you, nor can you say when it stopped. You should be able to remember, right?

But I can't pinpoint an exact year. The whole deal just

sort of slipped away from me somehow without my noticing at all, which makes me sad.

I watch Mrs. Shanahan stride down the hall. She seems bouncy, like my compliments validated her self-worth and made her feel as though her career is actually germane.[28]

And then she's gone.

---

28 I try to imagine being married to Mrs. Shanahan, eating root beer lollipops for every meal. Having a guidance counselor for a wife—she'd probably take good emotional care of me, or maybe she'd be so tired of taking care of people all day that when she came home from work she'd just be a selfish bitch. I can't decide which I believe. Probably the latter, I think.

SEVENTEEN
LETTER FROM THE FUTURE NUMBER 3

Hi, Daddy!

It's S, your daughter. This is so weird! I don't under-stand why I have to write you because you just left on the boat with Papa, and Horatio the dolphin was there, like always, to keep you company.

Momma says you're sad, but she also says that we're writing to you when you were a little boy, which I don't really understand. She makes me do a lot of strange school assignments, so I guess this is just another of those. You tell me to listen to Momma, so I do. She's helping me write the letter. She says I should tell you things you already know about me, which seems dumb, but here it goes.

My favorite color is dolphin gray.

My favorite constellation is Cassiopeia, because it's so much fun to say!

My favorite food is corn chowder with bacon. (Ha-ha! Joke!)

My favorite game is Who lived here? I love listening to the stories you make up about what it was like to live in the city underwater—what you call Philadelphia.

Once we found an apartment in an old skyscraper you called Liberty Place and you told me how some people used to live like kings and queens in the sky, looking down on all the people who had to live near the ground, but now you have to be really rich to live on the ground these days, which you said is ironic.

We went through the home and found dresses that proved a queen had lived there. The dresses were shiny and colorful. There were so many! And you said your mother had designed one of them, which was nice because you never talk about your mom.

And we found a chest of gold jewelry in the bedroom too. You let me keep the gold we found. We've been collecting gold from chests like that all over Outpost 37. I keep it under my bed just for fun in old poly-frozen food containers, although I really don't understand why people in the past loved gold so much, other than it's shiny. You call me a princess and sometimes we put on as much gold as we can, and you call me "Jay-Z," and then laugh so hard.

My favorite bedtime story is Philadelphia Phyllis, the little girl who used to solve crime mysteries back at the turn of the century. You tell me so many Phila-delphia Phyllis stories, and my favorite is the one where she stops a bully from picking on kids at school when she finds a magical weapon that gives her power. I often wish there were other kids here, but your stories about bullies make me wonder if I'm lucky it's only me.

My favorite song is the one your dad wrote called "Underwater Vatican," which you sing for me some-times, because you miss your dad. (Mom helped me spell Vatican and says it's where some important guy used to live but she couldn't really explain why he was important. She says we don't have guys like him anymore.)

Daddy, I can't think of anything else to write.

I love you.

I'm sorry that you were sad when you were a little boy, but you're hardly ever sad now, which is good, right?

Momma says I should tell you to hold on.

Hold on to what? I wonder.

I don't know.

But hold on.

There, I wrote that. Mom better give me full credit for this assignment.

Can't wait to see you at dinner tonight. I think we are having corn chowder with bacon *AGAIN*, because that's what we have the most of, so we have to save the other types of food for special occasions like birthdays, and mine's coming up in a week or so. You said you have a really special surprise for me.

I wonder what it is!

You never ever forget my birthday and you always make it special.

Is it true you don't have a birthday, like you said?

I wish I knew when your birthday was, because I would find you the best birthday present ever. Horatio would help me search Outpost 37 until we had the perfect prize.

Why won't you tell me when your birthday is?

Mom says it has to do with bad memories.

Why don't I have any bad memories? I ask her, and she says it's because I have such a good dad.

That makes me smile.

You are a good dad!

Love ya!

S, your "Jay-Z Princess"
(What is a "Jay-Z"? You never tell me!)

EIGHTEEN

Herr Silverman stands tall at six foot three or so. His body type would best be described as wiry. His hair is prematurely salt-and-pepper, and in ten years or so it will be entirely silver, at which point his last name will be appropriate. He always wears a solid-color tie; a long-sleeve white shirt; green, tan, or black pants with no pleats; black or brown suede lace-up shoes with a clunky heel; and a leather belt to match his shoes. Simple, but elegant—and most days he looks like a waiter at a fancy restaurant. Today he has on black pants, tie, shoes, and belt, and has shaved the beginnings of a goatee.[29]

At the beginning of every class he greets all of his students at the door, shakes everyone's hand on the way in, smiles

---

29 Herr Silverman is forever experimenting with facial hair. Last week he had an ill-advised Abraham Lincoln beard going. Students make comments about his various facial-hair stylings, but he never gets mad. He returns their digs with this smile that is more like a wink. It's like he's immune to the comments of other people, which I think is admirable.

at you, and looks you in the eye. He's the only teacher who does this, and the process often creates a human snake in the hallway. Sometimes the handshaking takes so long that there are still people lined up after the bell has rung, and this pisses off the other faculty members something awful.

Once our principal saw the line and yelled, "Get to class, all of you!" because he didn't see Herr Silverman in the door.

Herr Silverman said, "It's okay. We're just in the middle of our daily greeting. Everyone deserves a hello. Hello, Andrew."

Our principal made this really weird face, finally said, "Hello," and then walked away fast.

Today, when Herr Silverman shakes my hand, he smiles and says, "I like your new hat, Leonard."

It makes me feel so good, because I believe he really likes it, or rather he likes the fact that I'm expressing myself—that I'm wearing something no one else is wearing, and I'm not afraid to be different.[30]

"Thanks," I say. "Can I speak with you after class? I have something for you."

"Certainly." He nods and gives me an additional smile— a real smile, the kind that uses all the muscles in your face but doesn't look forced. Herr Silverman's smiles always make me feel better for some reason.

"Why does he have to shake everyone's hand every day?"

---

30 That's basically the mantra of Herr Silverman's teaching—think for yourself and do what's right for you, but let others do the same.

this kid Dan Lewis says about Herr Silverman as we take our seats.

"He's *so* fucking weird," Tina Whitehead answers under her breath.

And I want to pull out the P-38 and blast them both in their übermoronic heads, because Herr Silverman is the one teacher who cares about us and takes the time to let us know that— every day—and these stupid asshole classmates of mine hold it against him. It's like people actually *want* to be treated poorly.

Although once when we were talking after class, Herr Silverman told me that when someone rises up and holds himself to a higher standard, even when doing so benefits others, average people resent it, mostly because they're not strong enough to do the same. So maybe Dan Lewis and Tina Whitehead are just weaker than Herr Silverman and really need his kindness because of that, but I certainly wouldn't take the time to look them in the eye and smile every day if they talked like that behind *my* back. Herr Silverman is smart enough to realize that being different has consequences. He's always talking about that in class. Consequences. But he never bitches about the consequences he has to deal with, which makes him stand out.

"So," Herr Silverman says to the class, and I notice that once again he has refrained from rolling up his sleeves. "It's ethical-question day. Who has a question?"

We do this thing where someone asks a hard question related to the Holocaust—one with no clear right or wrong solution, like a moral dilemma—and then the class debates the answer.

Mine is the only hand in the air today, and so Herr Silverman says, "Leonard?"

"Let's just say that an American teenager inherited a real Nazi gun from his grandfather, who captured and executed a high-ranking Nazi officer. What should be done with the gun?"

I'm really curious to hear how my classmates respond. I'm sure their answers won't match mine. It's amazing how different they are from me.

Also, it's sort of thrilling to mess with their heads—to see how stupid they are, because they would never dream I have a gun, even though I basically just told them I do. Tomorrow they will look back on this discussion in a very different light, and they will realize just how unbelievably moronic they are.

This girl Lucy Becker is the first to answer, and she basically says that my gun belongs in the Holocaust museum in DC, and makes a speech about the importance of documenting our mistakes so we are not doomed to repeat them.[31]

"Counterpoint?" Herr Silverman says.

This kid Jack Williams who is kind of smart and interesting argues that the gun should be destroyed and talks about the rise of neo-Nazis who collect such things. Jack argues that if all Nazi propaganda were destroyed, no one would be

---

31 This is probably the standard answer that would score you the top mark on the essay portion of the SAT.

able to use it to recruit new Nazis. "That's why President Obama buried Osama bin Laden at sea," Jack says. "So no one could use his grave as a symbol."

"Very interesting rebuttal, Jack," Herr Silverman says. "Responses from the class?"

Kids in my class go back and forth about what to do with the gun, and—even though I asked the question—their answers start to freak me out a little. I mean I have a real Nazi gun in my backpack and everyone is talking about what to do with it, only they don't know that my hypothetical ethical question was real—they don't know that I have the gun on me right now.

They are all so remarkably stupid—but still, I start to worry that maybe one of them will put it together and guess why I asked that question on this particular day, and then they'll all lynch me.[32]

I worry so much that I start to sweat in my seat.

I feel really mixed up, and it's like I just want it all to end—everything.

And yet at the same time, I want someone to figure it out, to piece together all the hints I've been dropping all day long, for years and years even, but no one ever figures it out, and I'm beginning to see why people go mad and do awful

---

32 You may think that lynching is a means to an end if I wish to die, and I do, but being ripped apart limb by limb by übermoronic classmates is hardly a picturesque way to go. Death by übermorons is überunappealing.

things—like the Nazis and Hitler and Ted Kaczynski and Timothy McVeigh and Eric Harris and Dylan Klebold and Cho Seung-Hui all[33] did and so many other horrific people whom we learn about in school and—*You know what?* Fuck Linda for forgetting my birthday—**FUCK HER**—because how do you forget giving birth to someone eighteen years ago today and IRRESPONSIBLE and IRRESPONSIBLE and selfish and culpable and inhumane and—

"Leonard?" Herr Silverman says.

Everyone has turned his or her head and is looking at me.

"Concluding thoughts?"

I'm supposed to summarize the points of view regarding what to do with the P-38 and say which side I think won the debate, but I haven't been listening and I can't exactly say what I really think.

"I don't know. I just don't know anything today," I say, and then accidentally sigh.

Herr Silverman looks into my eyes until I look back into his and then I sort of plead with him using mental telepathy, thinking, *Please just move on. It's my birthday. I only have a few more hours on this planet. Please. Be kind. Let me off the hook.*

"It's a hard question, Leonard. A good one. I don't know either," Herr Silverman says, totally saving me.

_____

33 You should read about all of those killers. They all have a lot in common. I bet they felt lonely in many ways, helpless, FORGOTTEN, ignored, alienated, irrelevant, cynical, and sad. Read about them. You really should. You can learn a lot. More than I can explain here.

The übermorons roll their eyes and exchange glances.

He moves on to the lecture part of the class, discussing the concept of doubling, or being two different people at once—the good WWII German dad who eats a civilized dinner with his family at a formal table and reads bedtime stories to his children before he kisses their foreheads and tucks them into bed, all after spending the entire day ignoring the screams of Jewish women and children, gassing away, and heaving corpses into awful mass graves.

Basically, Herr Silverman says that we can simultaneously be human and monster—that both of those possibilities are in all of us.

Some of the stupid kids argue with him, saying they aren't like the Nazis and never could be, because Herr Silverman says we all double in some ways. And everyone in the class knows exactly what he's talking about, even if they pretend they don't.

Like how the kids the teachers think are the nicest are really the kids who drink tons of alcohol on weekends and drive drunk and date-rape everyone all the time and are constantly making less popular and truly nice kids feel shitty about themselves. But these same awful students transform themselves in front of the adults in power, so they will get the good college letters of recommendation and special privileges. I've never once cheated on a test or plagiarized, and Herr Silverman is probably the only teacher in the building who would write me a college-recommendation letter if I wanted one.

Our valedictorian, Trish MacArthur, got character letters from the most popular teachers in the building, and every student at this school knows she throws the most insane parties, where booze and drugs are prevalent and cops are regular visitors—but since her dad is the mayor, they just say, "Keep the noise down." A kid OD'd at her house last year and ended up in the hospital. And, magically, Trish MacArthur's reputation among faculty members remained untarnished. She's in A.P. English with me and she offered me two hundred bucks to "help her" with her *Hamlet* paper. She batted her eyelashes at me, crossed her ankles, pushed her boobs together with her shoulders, and said, *"Please?"* all helpless, just like she does with the male faculty members. They love it too. That girl really knows how to get what she wants. I told her to fuck off, of course. Called her a "broken valedictorian" and a "sham," at which point she uncrossed her ankles, let gravity do what it would with her boobs, stopped blinking like her eyelids were butterfly wings, and in a gruff, age-appropriate voice, she said, "Do you even have a purpose here at this high school? You're useless, Leonard Peacock."

Then she flipped me off and walked away.

That's our valedictorian.

Our finest.

Trish MacArthur.

"How do you know what you would have done if you were forced by your government to commit crimes but you still wanted to be a good parent?" Herr Silverman says.

"Were the Germans evil or were they responding to the social and political climate of their day?"

My classmates are mostly baffled.

As I listen to their whiny answers and attempts to place themselves on high moral pedestals, I realize the gap between them and me is widening as we get older.

The lies are so vivid, they're beginning to burn out my retinas.

Today's lecture pisses off the übermorons big-time, like the truth always does. And yet it makes me feel comforted somehow, not because Nazi officers did horrible things, but because Herr Silverman is trying to expose what everyone else in the world hides at all costs.

It's a depressing reality, how my classmates make love to their ignorance, and I mostly tune out and wait for class to end so I can give Herr Silverman his present and be closer to the Leonard Peacock finish line.

NINETEEN

When the bell rings, I stay seated.

Herr Silverman dutifully stands by the door and says good-bye to each student as he or she leaves.

I can tell he cares about everyone—even the stupidest among us.

It's like he's a saint or something.

Most kids rush out without even making eye contact, although Herr Silverman tries to give everyone his or her own individual good-bye.

It makes a difference, let me tell you, even if the über-morons in my class don't appreciate it.

There have been days when Herr Silverman was the only person to look me in the eye.

The only person all day long.

It's a simple thing, but simple things matter.

"So," Herr Silverman says as he closes the door.[34] "You wanted to speak with me."

"About that question I asked in class today," I say.

He sits down at the desk next to mine and says, "Ah, what to do with the Nazi gun."

"Yeah. Do you think it's possible to turn an object with a negative, horrible connotation into something that has a positive connotation?"

"Sure," he says.

I expect him to say more but he doesn't, which makes me feel flustered and unsure of what I should say next, so I reach into my backpack and pull out a small box, wrapped in pink. "This is for you."

Herr Silverman smiles and says, "Why do I get a present?"

"I'll tell you after you open it."

"Okay," he says, and then begins to peel off the pink paper very carefully. He opens the little box, looks up, raises his eyebrows, and says, "Is this what I think it is?"

"Yeah, it's the Bronze Star medal my grandfather was awarded for killing some high-ranking Nazi back in World War Two."

---

34 Most teachers refuse to close the door when they are alone with a student, saying it's against the law or something, which is pretty stupid. It's like everyone thinks teenagers are about to get raped every second of the day and that an open door can protect you. (It can't. How could it?) But Herr Silverman closes the door, which makes me trust him. He doesn't play by their rules; he plays by the right rules.

"Why are you giving this to me?"

"Well, for a lot of reasons. Most of which I can't really explain properly. That's why people give presents, right? Because they don't know how to express themselves in words, so you give gifts to symbolically explain your feelings. I got to thinking that the world would be a better place if they gave medals to great teachers rather than just soldiers who kill their enemies in wars. And with all the talk of World War Two in here and trying to make sense of horrible things, well, I just thought that I could turn the negative aspect surrounding that medal to a positive by giving it to you. Maybe that doesn't make any sense. I don't know. But I want you to have it, okay? It's important to me. Maybe you can keep it in your desk drawer and whenever you get to feeling like maybe teaching isn't worth it anymore you can think of that crazy kid Leonard Peacock who loved your class and gave you his grandfather's Bronze Star as a reward for being an excellent teacher. Maybe it will help you keep going. I don't know."

"I'm honored, Leonard—truly," he says, looking me in the eyes all serious, like he does. "But why did you give this to me *today*?"

"No reason, I guess. Today seemed like a good enough day," I lie, but my words sound shaky.

"Do you have your grandfather's gun from World War Two?" he asks, which freaks me out.

"What?" I say, all surprised, and suddenly I realize I'm inking my name into the desk.

I wonder why I'm doing that.

Then I wonder why Herr Silverman isn't telling me to stop graffitiing on school property.

"I'm just going to say this, Leonard, and I hope you won't take offense. Sudden changes in appearance. You did cut your hair, right?"

I just keep inking my name into the desk over and over again.

"Giving away treasured possessions. These are clear signs. Suicidal people often do these things. I'm worried you might be at risk."

L – E – O – N – A – R – D – P – E – A – C – O – C – K

L – E – O – N – A – R – D – P – E – A – C – O – C – K

L – E – O – N – A – R – D – P – E – A – C – O – C – K

I keep tracing the letters into the desk.

Why?

I've never written my name on a desk before.

"Are you trying to tell me something here today?" he says.

"Not really," I say without looking up. "I just wanted you to know how much your class means to me."

He doesn't say anything, but I can feel him looking at my face—I can tell he's concerned in a way that maybe no one else is, and that I'm going to have to do some acting if I want to make it out of here and complete my mission.

I reach down deep within myself and put on the Hollywood face once more. I smile at him, force a laugh, and say, "I probably *would* want to kill myself if I didn't get to spend time in this room every day. *I really would.* Your class is probably the only thing keeping me alive."

"That's not true. There's a lot for you to live for. Good things are definitely in your future, Leonard. I'm sure of it. You have no idea how many interesting people you'll meet after high school's over. Your life partner, your best friend, the most wonderful person you'll ever know is sitting in some high school right now waiting to graduate and walk into your life—maybe even feeling all the same things you are, maybe even wondering about you, hoping that you're strong enough to make it to the future where you'll meet. Did you ever write those letters, after we talked the last time? Letters from the future? Did you give it a try?"

"No," I lie, because writing those letters made me pretty emotional and I don't want to go there right now. I have to focus on the task at hand. "Maybe I'll do that tonight."[35]

"You should. I think it would help."

I get to thinking about the mystery again. I'm not really sure why—maybe because this is the last chance I'll get—but I say, "Can I ask you a personal question, Herr Silverman?"

"Okay."

---

35 Of course I've already written these letters, but just haven't shown Herr Silverman because the words are too intense and personal and insane—and maybe not what he wanted me to write. And yet, I feel like the letters are really important. I'm just not sure why and so I don't want to risk ruining the words. If Herr Silverman said the letters were wrong, I don't think I could handle it. Especially because he keeps saying the letters can save me, which means he believes I definitely need saving.

We sit there in silence for a few seconds as I try to work up the courage. My voice sounds shaky when I finally speak. "Why don't you ever roll up your sleeves or wear a short-sleeve shirt? Why don't you wear the faculty polo shirt on Fridays either?"

My heart's pounding hard enough to crack ribs because I kind of believe the answer might be able to save me. Even though that doesn't make any sense.

"You noticed that, huh?" Herr Silverman says.

"Yeah. I've been wondering for a long time now."

His eyes narrow slightly and then he says, "I'll make you a deal. You write those letters from the future and I'll tell you why I never roll up my sleeves. What do you say?"

"Sure," I say, and smile, because I can tell Herr Silverman really thinks the letter writing will help. He's passionate about helping fucked-up students like me. And for a moment I forget I already wrote the letters and won't be around after today—that I'll never know why Herr Silverman won't roll up his sleeves. "Do you like your gift?"

He picks up the Bronze Star and holds it in front of his face. "I'm very honored that you think so much of my teaching, but I'm not sure I can keep this, Leonard." He puts it back into the box and says, "It's a family heirloom. It's your birthright."

"Can you just keep it for me in your desk until I decide what I want to do with it?" I say, because I don't feel like arguing about this. "Just for a night at least. It would mean a lot to me."

"Why?"

"Just because. Okay?" I plead with my eyes.

"Okay," he says. "Just for a night. You'll be here tomorrow to pick it up? *Promise?*"

I know what he's doing—giving me an assignment that requires me to be here tomorrow. It actually makes me feel good, and I'm surprised by the fact that I can still feel better sometimes.

"Yeah," I lie. "I'll be here tomorrow."

"Good. I look forward to getting your perspective every day. I'd be crushed if your seat ever became empty. *Über*-crushed."

We sort of lock eyes and I think about how Herr Silverman is the only person in my life who doesn't bullshit me, and is maybe the only one at my school who really cares whether I disappear or stick around. "The government should give you a medal for being a good teacher, Herr Silverman. I'm serious about that. They really should."

"Thank you, Leonard. Are you sure you're feeling okay? There's nothing else you'd like to discuss?"

"Yeah, I'm sure. I'm off to see my guidance counselor right now, actually. Mrs. Giavotella already reported my 'strange behavior.' I'm sure they'll be getting around to asking your professional opinion of my sanity. But I'm off to Guidance now. So even if I *were* messed up, super-counselor Mrs. Shanahan'll fix me straight with a root beer lollipop before I leave the building, so no worries, right?"

When I look up to see if he's buying my lie, I can tell he isn't. So I say, "I'm sorry I wrote on your desk. Do you want me to clean it?"

"If I give you my cell phone number will you promise to call me if you feel like you're going to kill yourself?"

"I'm not going to—"

"You can call anytime—day or night. Will you promise to at least call me first, so I can tell you the reason I never roll up my sleeves? I bet knowing the answer to that question will make you feel better, but let's save it for when you're feeling really bad. It will be an emergency anecdote antidote," he says, and then smiles in a way that makes me smile, because he's proud of his stupid slant rhyme and he's also breaking the rules again, giving me his cell phone number. No other teacher in the building would do this. He's going above and beyond for me. And it makes me so sad to think he'll be really upset when he hears about my murder-suicide. "So will you promise me that you'll call if it gets worse—before you do anything rash? I'll tell you the answer if you call. It's a big secret. But I'll tell *you*, Leonard, because I think you need to know. You're different. And I'm different too. Different is good. But different is hard. Believe me, I know."

His saying that bit about being different sort of shocks me, because I never really thought about teachers feeling the way I sometimes do here at school, but I'm nodding seriously like I understand what he's telling me, and all the while I'm wondering what the hell is under his shirtsleeves.

He writes his cell phone number down in green ink, hands me the slip of paper, and says, "Write the letters from the future, Leonard. Those people want to meet you. Your life is going to get so much better. I promise you that. Just hold on as best you can—and believe in the future. Trust me. This is only a small part of your life. A blink. And if you find that you aren't able to believe it, call me anytime and we'll talk. I'll answer your question then. Just as soon as you need it. I promise."

"Why are you being so nice to me?" I say.

"People should be nice to you, Leonard. You're a human being. You should expect people to be nice. Those people in your future, the ones who are writing letters to you—they will be nice. Imagine it and it will be so. Write the letters."

I say, "Okay. Thanks, Herr Silverman," and then I get the hell out of there.

If only the world were full of Herr Silvermans. But it isn't. It's mostly full of übermorons like the majority of my classmates and sprinkled with sadistic assholes like Asher Beal.

I don't go to Guidance.

No root beer lollipop today.

I have one present left to deliver.

I have a mission to complete.

TWENTY

The last good birthday celebration Asher Beal and I had was seven or so years ago, back before all the really bad stuff started to happen.

At his party, when he unwrapped his present from me, he found a piece of paper with a question mark on it.

"What's this?" he said, squinting.

The sound of wooden pins being struck by bowling balls echoed through the alley. His oblivious but kind mother had booked two lanes.[36]

"Just the best birthday present you'll ever receive," I said.

"I don't get it," Asher said.

I remember the other kids at the party giving me strange

---

36 Asher and I had that in common—oblivious mothers.

looks—like what the fuck kind of present is a question mark on a piece of paper?[37]

"You will," I said confidently.

"When?"

"Soon."

"*Okay*," Asher said, shrugged, and then opened the gifts other kids had brought—WWE DVDs, video games, gift cards—typical stuff.

I remember feeling proud—like I was taking care of my best friend in a way that would blow his mind. Everyone else's mom just thoughtlessly bought generic presents that any eleven-year-old kid would forget about in a few days.

I invited Asher to spend the night at my house that weekend, and when he arrived, thinking we were just going to play video games and eat pizza, my dad came in and—employing this funny voice—said, "Mr. Beal, your car is ready."

"What?" Asher said, and then laughed. He was confused, had no clue, which made me so happy.[38]

Because my dad was in a good mood,[39] he pretended to be our hired driver, keeping his face blank, like he didn't know us, when he said, "Mr. Peacock has arranged for me to drive

---

37 I was already weird back then, and people were starting to notice more and more. Asher had lots of friends, but I really only had Asher.

38 Why is it that we love surprising people? Is it because we like to know something they don't? Does it give us a sense of power over others? Was I happy because I was controlling Asher? Or was I simply just trying to do something nice?

39 My dad was always in a good mood when he was about to gamble.

you to Atlantic City, where you will attend a rock 'n' roll concert this evening."

Asher's eyes lit up. "Don't even tell me you got Green Day tickets. *Did you?*"

I smiled and said, "Happy birthday."

His face exploded. "Yes! Yes! Yes!" he said, pumping his fists in the air, and then he sort of hugged and tackled me onto the couch.

I don't think I've ever felt better than I did at that moment, maybe because I've never made another human being *that* kind of I-will-joyfully-tackle-you happy.

The entire ride to Atlantic City, Asher talked about Green Day and what they'd probably play and how he just wanted to hear "American Idiot," because that was his favorite song. It was going to be his first official concert. I sat next to him, listening, feeding off his excitement.

My dad took us to an Irish pub for dinner and drank a few pints before he escorted us to the concert, which was in one of the casinos. I can't remember which one because they all look the same to me. When Asher realized we had front-row seats, he hugged me again and said, "You're the man, Leonard Peacock! Seriously! First row? First row? *How?*"

My dad still had connections back then, but I didn't say that. I just sort of shrugged modestly.

It felt so fucking good making my friend happy.

Like I was a hero.

Green Day came on and performed.

When they played "American Idiot," Asher grabbed my biceps, screamed in my face, and then sang every word.

I was never a big Green Day fan, but it was the best concert I've ever attended, mostly because it was so much fun to see Asher experience *his* favorite band live—knowing that I made it happen, that I was the hero that night, that I'd given him the perfect present, and all those assholes at his birthday party—all the kids in our class who squinted at the question mark I drew on a piece of paper—just didn't get it, me, or life in general.

Wearing Green Day concert shirts featuring heart-shaped grenades, we met my dad afterward at the designated place right outside the casino floor and I could hardly hear him when he asked about the show because my ears were ringing.

"It rocked!" Asher kept saying. "So awesome!"

"All right, all right," Dad said all cool, like he used to whenever he'd had a few drinks and his eyes were glassy. "All right, all right." He'd say it fast and sort of rhythmic, putting the accent on the second *ri* and dropping the last *t*, so it sounded like "all-right, all-*rye*."

Toward the end of our time together, when Dad really went off the deep end, you could say anything to him and he'd say, "All-right, all-*rye*." "Dad, I failed Earth Science." "All-right, all-*rye*." "Mom's banging this French fashion designer she used to model for." "All-right, all-*rye*." "I just lit your balls on fire, Dad." "All-right, all-*rye*." He became one of those dolls that repeat a catchphrase every time you pull its string. "All-right, all-*rye*." "All-right, all-*rye*." "All-right, all-*rye*."

In our hotel room my dad said, "You guys can rent a movie, but stay in the room. *All-right, all-rye?* I'm going back down to the floor. Feeling lucky tonight," which was no surprise, because my dad was always leaving me alone, even when I was a kid.

Asher and I watched the clock for ten minutes after my dad left, just long enough for him to start gambling, before we began exploring the hotel.

We ran down the endless mazelike hallways, knocking on the doors we passed, emptying the ice machines and having ice-ball fights in the stairwell; took turns sitting in the maid's cart and pushing each other into walls; tried to sneak into an after-hours dance club and got caught by the bouncer, who laughed his ass off when—with straight faces—we told him it was Asher's twenty-first birthday. We searched the casino floor for the members of Green Day and got kicked out, scarfed down some late-night pizza, and ended up sitting on the boardwalk with our elbows on the railing and our feet dangling over the side.

"Man, this night was the shit!" Asher said. "Best birthday present ever. Hands down."

"Yeah, you know it," I remember saying as we listened to the waves crashing somewhere in the darkness.

"Do you think we'll come back to this hotel when we're adults?" Asher asked. "Do you think we'll still be hanging out?"

If you would have put my grandfather's Nazi P-38 handgun

to my eleven-year-old head, told me to tell the truth or die, and then asked me if Asher and I would be best friends for life, I would have said yes on that night without hesitation.[40]

"Probably," I said, and then we just sat dangling our feet off the boardwalk.

We really didn't say much more than that; nothing all that extraordinary happened—just typical stupid-ass kid stuff.[41]

Maybe it was the type of high only kids can get and understand.

There were hundreds of adults drinking alcohol and gambling and smoking that night, but I bet none of them felt the high Asher and I did.

Maybe that's why adults drink, gamble, and do drugs—because they can't get naturally lit anymore.

Maybe we lose that ability as we get older.

Asher sure did.

---

40 Kids are like blind passengers—they just don't see what's coming down the road.
41 Did you ever think about all of the nights you lived through and can't remember at all? The ones that were so mundane your brain just didn't bother to record them. Hundreds, maybe thousands of nights come and go without being preserved by our memory. Does that ever freak you out? Like maybe your mind recorded all the wrong nights?

TWENTY-ONE

One day after a long, depressing afternoon wearing my funeral suit and studying miserable adults in Philadelphia, I exited my town's train station, and this girl[42] I had never seen before stuck a piece of paper in my face. Then she said, "The way, the truth, and the light!"

"Excuse me?" I said.

"Here's a tract. Read all about it."

I took the piece of paper, which was like a mini–comic book. The pictures and words were all in red ink, which looked dramatic and intense. On the front cover was a picture

---

42 What I noticed first was that she didn't look anything like the other girls in my high school. She was cat-faced and throwback-looking, like the old classic type of girls you see in Bogart films. More sophisticated. Mysterious. Dangerous. Femme fatales. The type that makes you risk being murdered by her enemies just so that you will eventually be able to kiss her as the string music cranks up and she's about to faint. The kind of girl for whom you happily lose your mind. She wasn't like the 1970s sunglasses femme fatale I had followed in Philadelphia to an unfortunate ending, I could tell. She seemed less manic, happier, brighter, kissable.

of a smiling man. Underneath his kind face were these words: *You can be the nicest guy in the world, but without Jesus in your heart, you are going to hell.*

I remember laughing when I read it, because it seemed so over the top—like a joke maybe. And I wondered if this throwback-looking girl was playing some sort of game—like this was just part of her spiderweb, her trap.

"Who are you?" I said, trying to sound cool and collected and Bogie-like.

"My name is Lauren Rose. And I'm here to show you the way. Tell you the good news."

Her name was Lauren and she was a tall blond.

Lauren.

If I were the type of person who believed in signs, I would have been a little freaked, because she actually looked very much like a youngish version of Lauren Bacall, a tall blond who was also cat-faced, and was devastatingly beautiful in her prime—irresistible. And after watching Bogie win Bacall so many times in black-and-white Hollywood land, I felt a sort of inevitability. This would be the first girl I would kiss. I declared it in my mind—set the goal, and then I locked on like a greyhound chasing a rabbit.

"What good news?" I asked, trying to sound as calm, suave, and confident as black-and-white Bogie—pretending that we were in *The Big Sleep*. "Because I sure could use some."

"That Jesus Christ died for your sins."

"Oh."

I didn't know how I felt about that, and her selling religion seemed to snap me out of the scene for a moment, but I had already set the goal—and I knew that Bogie always gets Bacall no matter what the odds, no matter how many bad guys are in his way. So I tried to change the subject.

"I don't think I've seen you before. Do you go to high school here in town?"

"No, I don't," she said to me, and then said, "Jesus loves you," to a group of businessmen who ignored her and the tract she was trying to hand them. They didn't even look at her. It was like she was invisible. And while I'm not really one for getting into debates with religious people either, I felt bad for Lauren, because she had this desperate look in her eyes— the kind that needs someone else to make it go away. I imagined she was invisible to most commuters, who only wanted to go home after a long day of work, which I knew from many hours of observation.

I mean—there are people who believe in one of the various gods available already and therefore don't need the tract, and then there are people who will never believe in this sort of thing. And I imagine the gals and guys in between mostly aren't interested in being harassed on their way to and from work.

"Where do you go to school?" I asked, hoping to change the subject.

"Oh, I'm homeschooled."

"So your mom teaches you?"

"And my dad. Yes."

She kept looking eagerly at the people coming out of the subway station and wasn't really paying me much attention anymore, which I thought was weird, since I was the only person who had taken her pamphlet. You'd think she'd concentrate on winning me over, right? She was a classic femme fatale—determined, gorgeous, a real dame.

"Why?" I said.

"Why what?"

"Why are you homeschooled?"

"My parents want me to have a Christian education."

"What's that?" I said, just to keep the conversation going.

"An education rooted in the Bible."

"Oh."

"Jesus loves you," she said to an old man who ignored her outstretched pamphlet.

"If I read this," I said, holding up the story she gave me, "can we talk about it afterward?"

She turned to face me and her eyes lit up. "Are you serious? You'll really read it and consider giving your life to Jesus Christ?"

"Sure," I said, and then laughed. I must have been the first person who ever agreed to read her tracts. She was acting like a little excited kid, but she had to be about my age—and yet she seemed so much younger, maybe unspoiled, like she could still get really excited about something in public without trying to hide it. Even though she was getting excited about Jesus, I liked the fact that she was genuinely keyed up about anything.

She said, "Do you want to come to my church this Sunday?"

"Let me read this and we can talk about it."

"How will you contact me afterward?" she said, looking very concerned.

"I'm going to read it on that bench over there and then we can talk, okay?"

She bit down on her bottom lip and nodded way too enthusiastically—like it sort of creeped me out—and if she wasn't doing that cat-eye thing that Lauren Bacall sometimes does in Bogie films, the thing where she squints sophisticatedly and looks up at her man from under her eyebrows or seductively out of the corners of her eyes, I probably would have left right then.

When I started toward the bench, she said, "Oh, wait," and then began shuffling through her papers. She smiled and said, "Read this one instead," and extended a new pamphlet toward me. "It's for teenagers."

"Okay." I sat down on the bench and read it in about five minutes.

It was sort of unbelievable.

Actually, it was a little insane—and should have been my cue to get the hell away from this dame.

The basic gist is that there are four teenagers in a convertible, out "cruising"—two guys, two girls. They go to the woods to "park," which I gather basically means to drink beer, make out, and feel each other up. The protagonist of the pamphlet is the boy in the backseat, who is a "born-again Christian" and feeling a bit conflicted about the "sins" that are happening. In the little bubble over the kid's head it said something like, "Cindy is so beautiful and I really want to go all the way with her, but I know Jesus would be disappointed in me. I already let him down by drinking beer."[43]

At one point you get the protagonist's view of the front seat—it's one of those old-style front seats that's like a bench with no space in between the driver and passenger, or no center console, which makes me think this is a very old tract—maybe from the 1950s. And we see the girl's naked ankles sticking up in the air, which I guess means the couple in the front is having sex. Cindy, the girl in the backseat, says to the protagonist, "You know you wanna. Let's have some fun. Didn't your mother ever tell you to try new things?"

The next frame shows protagonist Johnny chugging a beer.

And then we see them driving home and the driver's eyes are slits, which I assume means he is drunk.

We get a close-up of Johnny's face next, and the bubble

---

43 The scenario is complete bullshit, because the girl he's "parking" with keeps feeling his inner thigh, and he keeps pushing her hand away. No way a teenage boy pushes some girl's hand away from his crotch when he thinks she's attractive. Also, everyone knows Jesus drank wine with his buddies, so why would he be disappointed in a beer drinker?

over his head reads, "I let you down, Jesus. Sex. Booze. I'm so so sorry. Can you ever forgive me?"

You won't believe this but the next frame shows the car crashing into a tree, and then we see Johnny's ghost floating up to heaven, which is when I figured out that he was dead. I was sort of happy that the other three teenagers lived at least, but I couldn't figure out the point of the story.

The pamphlet shows a sober Johnny in heaven speaking with Jesus, who has a typical Jesus beard and white robe and halo, but Jesus kind of looks like a professional baseball player to me and I'm not sure why. He has that baseball-player look with shaggy hair and a beard, but he's clean-cut at the same time. Not like a hillbilly or anything. Do you know what I mean?

"I'm so sorry I let you down, Jesus," Johnny says.

"You asked forgiveness and I have forgiven you because you are a Christian," Jesus said, which I thought was pretty nice.

"Thank you for sparing the lives of my friends," Johnny says.

Jesus gets this really sad look on his face, which lets you know that the friends didn't live, and I almost stopped reading right there, because I was pretty sure I knew what sort of bullshit was coming. "Why didn't you tell your friends about me before they died?" Jesus says. "You had so many opportunities."

"My friends *died*?" Johnny says with this horrible look on his face.

The next frame shows the three other teenagers screaming and holding their faces as a sea of flames burns and engulfs them.

"They could be here in heaven right now with you, Johnny, but you didn't tell them about me," Jesus says.

Johnny puts his head in his hands and weeps.

Then there are numbers you can call and websites too, all of which will help you give your life to Jesus.

Jesus Christ! I thought.

It was a wild story, and I was mostly confused, so I walked over to Lauren and said, "I'm not sure I get it."

This awful, anxious look bloomed on her face and she said, "You don't want to go to hell, do you?"

I was going to say I don't believe in hell, but I was determined to kiss Lauren Bogie-style, so I didn't want to say anything that would end the conversation. I had seen enough Bogie films to know that you have to ride out the insanity when it comes to beautiful women, and even with all the crazy talk, Lauren seemed to get more and more attractive every time I looked at her. Also, this was the longest conversation I'd had with a girl my age, so I didn't want to blow it.

I asked, "Why didn't Johnny go to hell if he had sex and drank, just like the others?"

"He asked Jesus into his heart."

"What do you mean?"

"No matter what you've done, if you ask Jesus into your

heart, you get to go to heaven. The blood of Jesus Christ washes our hearts clean as snow."

"So you just have to say magic words?"

"What?"

"If you say, 'Jesus come into my heart,' you are covered? You get to go to heaven then. That's it?"

"You have to *mean* it."

"How can you tell if you mean it?"

"You know in your heart, and God knows. What's in *your* heart?" Lauren pointed at my chest.

"I don't know," I said, because my heart was full of desire. I wanted to kiss Lauren like the girl kissed Johnny in the car. I wanted to "park" with Lauren in the worst way. That's what my heart was telling me.

"Do you want to come to my church this Sunday?" Lauren asked.

"Will you be there?"

"Of course! My father's the pastor. You can sit with me in my family's pew, right up front!"

I didn't want to go to any church, but I knew going would help my cause, so I said, "Okay, then."

That Sunday I went to Lauren's church, which I had walked by a million times without even giving it—or what it stood for—a thought. It was a medieval-looking stone building with an impressive steeple, a classic bell tower, circular stained-glass windows, red cushions on wooden pews, and all the rest.[44]

The men inside were wearing suits and I had come in jeans and a sweater, which made me feel self-conscious, but no one said anything to me about it, which I thought was civilized of the churchgoers.

I found Lauren sitting in the front row with her mother, who was also a head-turner, like Lauren, which gave me high hopes for the day.[45]

They looked more like sisters than mother and daughter, and I wondered if believing in Jesus kept you younger-looking. But then I thought, if that were really true, Linda would be the biggest Jesus freak going, because she'd drown a baby in a bathtub if it would make her look ten years younger.

The best part about the church were the huge organ pipes at the back, up in the balcony, which were so loud you could almost see the air buzzing when the organist played. It made me feel like I had traveled back in time, that organ music, although I'm not really sure why.

Just to make things more interesting, I pretended that I was an anthropologist from the future sent back to observe what religious life was like in the past.

There were announcements about various church goings-

---

44 If you can believe it, this was the first time I had ever been to a church service other than funerals.
45 Beautiful women make any situation bearable.

on—like Bible study groups meeting at this or that time, and church dinners, and which people needed help, and who was in the hospital—which was nice, because it really made you feel like everyone took care of each other here, like they all were part of a gigantic family.

I could really see the appeal, for sure.

Next, everyone sang a few hymns—which was also kind of nice, because where else will you experience a few hundred people singing together?—and then Lauren's father gave a talk about humility and humbling ourselves so that we might be able to best serve God, which I didn't really understand.

If god existed and he created the whole universe, like these people believed, why would he need our help, let alone our praise?

Why would he need us to serve him?

Was god really both all powerful *and* emotionally needy?

It didn't really make any sense to me at all, and I knew I was going to have a hard time conveying this idea to my superiors in the future when I—being a time-traveling anthropologist— report on ancient religions.

There was more nice singing after that, and then we all waited in line to shake Lauren's dad's hand, because he was the head of this church.

So many people kissed Lauren's dad's ass—like he was a god himself—it took forever for the line to move.

When we got to the front, Pastor Rose patted my back and said, "Are you the fish my Lauren reeled in this week?"

Fish? I thought. This was getting even more bizarre.

"I guess so," I said, wondering why the hell he was wearing a graduation gown.

"You come to my office sometime and we'll talk man-to-man about the finer points of Christianity, okay?"

"I prefer speaking with Lauren," I said, and he gave me a look that let me know that was definitely the wrong answer.

"Well, when you get serious about Jesus, I'll be here. Young men like you need mentors, and that's a man's job, son. Lauren's a fine Christian young woman, no doubt. But she brought you to us for a reason. You come see me, okay?" He winked—I shit you not—and then shook the next person's hand, so Lauren and I moved on to lunch in this basement gym where tables and chairs had been set up and everything smelled of sweaty socks and pot roast.

"So what did you think?" Lauren asked me over plastic plates and red Solo cups.

Church was okay, I guess. I liked the singing part, and the organ. But mostly the whole thing just seemed sort of silly to me. I was smart enough not to say that to Lauren. Instead I went into Bogie mode and said, "You look very pretty in that dress." It was a deep violet number, knee-length, with spaghetti straps. She was like one of those exotic plants that lure insects into their sticky sweet traps and then eat them. When I looked at her, I wanted to be eaten.

"Thank you," she said. "So do you think you want to give your life to Jesus?"

I was just about to lie when this muscle-y blond football-player-looking kid snuck up behind Lauren and started to massage her shoulders. "Hey, buttercup," he said.

Buttercup? Really?

"Hey," Lauren said in a way that let me know this wasn't just any old church member. He looked like the Johnny kid in the pamphlet and nothing like me. "Leonard, this is my boyfriend, Jackson. Jackson, this is Leonard."

"I hear you're serious about making Jesus Christ your Lord and Savior," Jackson said to me. "It's definitely the way to go."

"Do you enjoy parking?" I asked, although I'm not sure why. Probably because I was angry and just wanted to leave. I felt so tricked by Lauren. Being eaten by her was one thing, but introducing me to her boyfriend after she'd led me on— that was entirely unacceptable. She used her femme fatale skills to get me into her church, bait-and-switch style, when she already had a boyfriend who was much more normal-looking than me—a completely different type. "Do you guys park?"

"*Leonard!*" Lauren said, because she definitely got the reference, although it took her a second.

"What are you talking about?" Jackson said, and made a confused face.

I looked up at the clock on the gym wall—I remember it was protected by mesh wire so basketballs wouldn't smash it.[46]

---

46 Weird what we remember and what we don't.

"Quarter to one already?" I asked, and then started to lie again, only these were escape lies. The Bogie-Bacall fantasy had been temporarily shattered, so I just wanted out of this church. "Holy shit! I have to roll my grandmother over in her bed. She gets bedsores if I don't do it every four hours or so. My grandfather does it when I'm at school, but he refuses to do it on the weekends. He says, 'The weekends are mine,' which seems mean until you know that he has Alzheimer's, so you really can't hold it against him. Okay. Off I go."

I stood up and walked out of the gym, up the stairs, and out into the afternoon.

Lauren followed me and kept saying, "Wait up. Let's talk. What's going on here? I thought you were serious about Jesus."

I spun around and said, "I'm a devout atheist. I don't believe in hell, so none of this scares me. I really just wanted to go parking with you, like the kids do in that pamphlet you gave me, because I think you're beautiful—like Lauren Bacall—and so unlike the girls at my school. And I sort of admire your standing at the train station all alone giving out pamphlets, trying to save people. You seemed so interesting when I met you—like no one else I had ever met before. But you don't seem the same in your church—like there's no risk being Christian here because everyone is Christian in your church. You're just one of many here, where at the train station you were one of a kind. And I'm a one-of-a-kind type of person, and that's just the way it is. So we're definitely breaking up. And I can't believe your boyfriend looks like Johnny from the pamphlet. Jesus Christ, you could do better!"

Lauren just stood there with her mouth open.

"I'm sort of crazy. I'm mostly lonely," I said, because she looked little-kid confused and I was starting to feel bad for her again. I guess I only liked her when we were alone. "I follow sad miserable-looking adults on the trains all day sometimes and so I thought we had weird train-station behavior in common and—"

"You all right, Lauren?" said Jackson, who was now somehow rubbing Lauren's shoulders again and glaring at me like he wanted to kill me before I could accept Jesus Christ into my heart, and would therefore—in his mind—end up burning in a sea of fire.

"She's all right," I said. "I'm leaving. Problem solved."

I left.

TWENTY-TWO

I'd see Lauren at the train station from time to time but she pretended like she didn't know who I was, and I pretended like I didn't know who she was either.

This went on for a year or so.

Then one day, I saw her in Center City being harassed by a bum, who was following her and yelling, "Give me a sandwich and you think you saved the world? It don't work like that! You think God sent you to give me two pieces of bread with a slice of cheese and a flimsy circle of bologna and cheap bright-yellow mustard and that's supposed to make up for ten years of living in a cardboard box? That's what you want me to believe? God loves me because you gave me a half-assed sandwich? I'm homeless—*not crazy!*"

The guy had wild eyes and a lion's mane of gray hair that made his head look like a frozen sun or something.

"I'm sorry I disturbed you," Lauren said.

"That ain't good enough," the bum said. "I gotta few

things you can tell your god the next time you pray in your nice warm house with a toilet in it and a whole refrigerator of food that you'd never give to bums like me because it costs too fucking much and so it ain't bum food. I bet you got a dog that eats better than me."

"I'm sorry," Lauren said. "I'm sorry."

It was kind of funny seeing Lauren getting verbally beat down by a bum, and I was totally on the bum's side, but Lauren looked so rattled that I had to intervene. And so I went up to the bum and said, "I was sent to you by the Atheist Society of America. We believe in chaos and no god at all, and want to congratulate you on putting this uppity Christian in her place. As a reward we'd like to give you twenty dollars that you may use to buy a superior sandwich or whatever you'd like. No strings attached."

The gray lion-haired bum looked at me like I was insane, but he snatched the money out of my hand and walked away.

"He's just going to buy alcohol or drugs, you know," Lauren said, which made me sad, because she didn't know that man at all, let alone whether he had a dependency problem.

"I don't believe we've met before. I'm Leonard Peacock," I said, and stuck out my hand confidently, putting on the Bogie charm.

"I remember who you are," Lauren said, ignoring my outstretched hand, playing hard-to-get Bacall again. She looked really shook up, so I didn't take offense. "Why do you think he got so angry at me?"

I didn't feel like listing all the reasons why she deserved the verbal beatdown from the homeless man—mostly because I knew that wouldn't help my cause—so I just changed the subject. "You're welcome."

"What?"

"You no longer have a bum trailing you, yelling at you."

"Oh," she said. "I was fine. God would have protected me."

"Maybe god sent me to protect you," I said, playing devil's advocate.

"Maybe."

"God says you should have coffee with me right now?"

"You want to have coffee with me? Why?"

"We can talk more about god," I said, giving her the line she wanted.

"What you said to Jackson and me at my church," Lauren said. "It was really *rude*."

"I know, I know. I'm sorry," I said just to get her to have coffee with me, because her face was all red from her being harassed, and she looked so femme fatale—so much like she needed saving—that I didn't even care she had *trap* written all over her.

"I'm not going to park with you," she said in this really serious way that depressed me; I only had so much Bogart in me, truth be told, and I was already running low.

"Do people in your church really use the word *park* as a euphemism for having sex in cars? Do teenagers really have sex in cars? I don't even drive."

"If you're just going to make fun of me for going to church and believing in God, I don't want to have coffee with you, Mr. Atheist."

Her calling me Mr. Atheist really deflated me because it felt like a wall—like my personal beliefs were going to keep us from being friends and ultimately kissing. It was like once again someone was labeling me and putting me in a box just as soon I expressed myself. Suddenly, the whole deal didn't feel like a game anymore.

Consequences, Herr Silverman says. Consequences.

I abandoned my plan. I made a real attempt. "I'm not going to make fun of you, okay? I just want to understand you. Maybe we can have an exchange? Maybe we can talk about our beliefs over coffee without trying to change each other. What do you think?"

"I'm not going to kiss you."

"You have Jackson to kiss, right?"

"I've never kissed Jackson either."

"I thought he was your boyfriend."

"I'm saving myself for my husband."

"Saving yourself?"

"Yep."

"So you won't even kiss someone before you get married?"

"Not the way you're thinking of kissing. A peck on the lips or cheek doesn't count."

I must say, her never having been kissed was really attractive to me for some reason. I'm not exactly sure why. Maybe I was drawn to Lauren's innocence. Maybe it reminded me of who I was before all the bad stuff went down.

I said, "You owe me one cup of coffee for getting the homeless man off your back. I know this place around the corner. What do you say?"

"We'll talk about our religious beliefs. Like an exchange, right?"

"Right."

And then we walked to this coffee shop that had crazy huge couches that were random geometrical shapes like triangles and rhombuses and circles. It was like being in a daycare room for giant babies.

We got a seat and I ordered a double espresso, because I thought that would sound really sophisticated and cool and was the most Bogart-like thing I could order since I couldn't order gin or scotch. Lauren ordered a peppermint mocha, which made her seem like a child again, and I also liked that about her,[47] so I called the waiter back and said, "I'll also have a peppermint mocha."

Lauren looked around the shop and up at the ceiling like she was examining the construction of it, making sure the roof wouldn't fall on our heads, and then said, "So why are you wearing a suit?"

_____

47 It was strange how I wanted her to be both a sexy Bacall-type figure and I also wanted her to be a kid at the same time, because those states are pretty much opposites, so she couldn't be both simultaneously.

"I do that sometimes when I take a day off school to do research."

"What are you researching?"

"Aging and the possibility of adult happiness."

"Jesus can make you happy."

I laughed and said, "Do you talk about anything else besides Jesus?"

Lauren smiled and said, "So why have you been ignoring me for a year?"

"I haven't. *You've* been ignoring *me.*"

"I have not been ignoring you! I try to catch your eye whenever I see you at the train station, but you walk by so quickly without looking. I've actually been quite hurt by your snubs."

I noted that she was doing the cat-face femme-fatale thing again. She was now back in trap mode. "What about Jackson?" I asked.

"What about him?"

"I bet he doesn't want you talking to me."

"He would be happy if we talked about God. He believes we should save everyone too."

"Then why doesn't he help you pass out Jesus pamphlets?"

"He used to, but he's at college now. And he's not my boyfriend anymore."

That bit of news got my heart pumping. "Is that why you're having coffee with me today? Because you no longer have a boyfriend?" I said, hoping for the right answer, but the waiter came back with our peppermint mochas.

Lauren sipped hers and said, "Yum!"

That made me smile. I sipped mine and it tasted just like a melted York Peppermint Pattie.

"Maybe I could take you to dinner sometime, what do you think?"

"Are you asking me out on a date?" Lauren said.

"Okay, scratch that," I said, because her eyebrows got all scrunchy and her eyes got all squinty, and not in the sexy cat-face Bacall way either. "Maybe this right here could be our first date, and then we won't have to worry about the asking and saying yes part. We could just start now."

"Well, I only date boys who are Christian."

"Oh," I said. "I see." I wasn't really that daunted at first because it seemed like such a silly thing to me—something we could easily overcome. I didn't realize how limiting her Christianity actually was.

"Do you want to talk about Jesus?" she asked.

"That's your favorite topic, huh?"

"Yep."

"Don't you have any other interests at all?"

"Sure. But we have to clear this hurdle before we move on to those. I don't want to waste your time or mine."

"But doesn't your religion tell you that *everyone* is important? I mean, that bum obviously didn't believe in Jesus and you still gave him a sandwich."

"Yeah, but I don't want to *date* him!" Lauren kind of

rolled her eyes at me all adorable and then sipped her pepper-mint mocha.

God, I loved her so much at that moment, mostly because she had just implied that she'd consider dating me—that my dating a girl was actually a possibility.

"Leave it to me to fall in love with a Jesus freak," I said, and then laughed to make it seem as though I was only being playful and kidding.

"You don't even know me," she said.

"But I'd like to."

She sighed and looked out the window.

Then we just sort of sipped our mochas and watched people pass outside for fifteen minutes or so.

Afterward, we walked to the train station together and then sat side by side on the ride back to Jersey. Our elbows were touching through our coats and that gave me an embar-rassing hard-on, which would have been a problem if it were summer and I had no coat to hide under.

I could sort of tell that she was feeling something too, regardless of whether she wanted to or not.

When we got off the train she made the Bacall cat face again and said, "It was nice having coffee with you. Maybe God will change your heart and we can continue our talk about Jesus. And then who knows?"

She said that in this really flirty way that made me even harder than I already was. My hands were in my peacoat pockets and I was sort of holding the stupid hard-on to my abdomen like a loaded and cocked catapult. I couldn't have spoken if you paid me so I just nodded.

"I'll be praying for you," Lauren said, and then waved good-bye by bending the tops of her right-hand fingers three times, just like a little kid would. She spun around and then walked away from me.

I kept thinking she was trying to trick me again—using her sexuality like female teachers do, flirting to control you. That she was nothing but a trap. But I had to know what it was like to kiss her. I just did. I didn't want to fake being interested in Christianity again, because I was so tired of faking it with everyone else in my life. So I decided to think long and hard about the possibility of god, since that was all Lauren wanted to discuss. I thought up a list of questions and I asked her a new one at the train station three times a week.

Why would god allow the Holocaust to happen?

If god made everything, why did he invent sin to trick us and then hold our sins against us?

Why are there so many religions in the world if god created the world and wants us to be Christian?

Why does god allow people to fight wars over him?

What if you were born in a different culture and never even heard of Jesus Christ—would god send you to hell for not being Christian? And if so, do you believe that's fair?

Why are men always the leaders in your church? Aren't

women capable of leading too? Isn't such a patriarchal system sexist in this day and age?

Why do so many babies die?

Why are there so many poor people in the world?

Did Jesus visit any other planets in distant unknown universes?

Stuff like that.

The next time we saw each other it was a warm spring afternoon and she was wearing these shorts with pockets on the sides and I couldn't stop looking at her creamy thighs, which were perfect. In front of the subway station, she was all smiles and said, "HELLO, LEONARD! I've been praying for you! God's given me a special peace regarding our friendship. I know it will be for a reason."

But the more questions I asked throughout the summer, the quieter and less enthusiastic she got, and the less I enjoyed studying her various exposed body parts.

It was like she thought I was beating her down with my words when all I really wanted to do—besides look at her wonderful body—was understand and have an honest conversation.

Lauren never really answered my questions, unfortunately. She just quoted Bible verses and repeated things her father had told her, but I got the sense that she didn't really believe the things she was saying so much as she was clinging to those answers because she didn't have any other answers and maybe having the *wrong* answers was better than having *no* answers.

I don't really know, but the more questions I asked, the more she started to hate me—I could tell—which was just so so depressing.[48] She also started to notice that I was checking her out, which got kind of awkward, especially when she started wearing these really baggy longer shorts, which ruined the view and sent me a pretty clear message.

The last time I saw her was maybe a week ago. When I walked up to her at the train station, she frowned and said, "If you want answers to your questions, you're going to have to speak with my father. He says your questions are dangerous and should be answered by a church elder."

That depressed the hell out of me.[49]

"Listen," I said as several sad briefcase-toting suits flocked by in a depressing, emotionless rush. "No more questions. I realize that maybe you and I are incompatible. I'm not going to harass you anymore, but can I ask you just one favor?"

"It depends," she said, looking me in the eyes in this way that could have been flirting or could have been leave me alone. It was hard to tell. "What do you want?"

"Will you keep praying for me?"

Her eyes got wide for a second—like she was really excited that I asked her to do that—but then her eyes shrunk

---

48 Why is it that people only like it when you ask questions that they have answered a million times and hate you for stumping them? I love questions that stump me. I really enjoy thinking about possible answers to those types of questions for days and days. Does anyone else like to ponder anymore, or am I just a total freak?
49 Religious pun?

into little black peas, and she said, "Don't make fun of me, okay?"

"What?"

"After listening to all of your weird, endless questions, I don't think you really believe in prayer, Leonard." Her voice was harsh, and reminded me of Linda's when she's "reached the end of her rope"[50] with me, like she's always saying.

"I'm going through some rough stuff I haven't told anyone about and it would really help if I thought you were praying for me," I said. "You can even lie if you want, but if you'd just say you'd continue to pray for me, I think I might be able to make it through this bad stuff, because at least I'd know one person was pulling for me in her own special way."

Lauren looked at me like she thought I might be tricking her, but then—without making the femme-fatale cat face—she said, "Okay. I'll pray for you. Every day. And I don't lie. Ever."

I smiled and walked away quickly before she could change her mind or say anything else that would convince me of her insincerity.

---

50 I looked up the origin of that "reaching the end of my rope" expression. The Internet told me that people used to say "at the end of my tether." And tether referred to the leashes of horses or dogs. So I guess the phrase is supposed to evoke the image of a dog running for a squirrel or something and then suddenly being jerked back by the rope tied around its neck. It's reached the end. It can't go any farther. So I guess I'm beyond Linda's reach now. Her tether is too short. Like she's told me over and over again. I wonder what the hell she's tethered to? NYC? Fashion? Jean-Luc? Take your pick. Lauren is tethered to religion.

Thinking about Lauren praying for me every day helped a lot at first; it really did.

But then after a few days, it stopped working—I know because I started to feel like I really wanted to kill Asher Beal again—which made me wonder if she had quit praying, and then as my desire to kill amplified, I convinced myself she definitely had.

TWENTY-THREE

Just like I'd hoped, after school today, when I arrive at our town's subway station, I find Lauren handing out tracts, or rather holding the tracts out to everyone who passes by and doesn't say a word to her or even give her a glance.

I wonder what crazy bit of propaganda she's peddling today and what scary pictures are inside—hell flames and bloody saviors and all sorts of Christian gore.

I didn't come here to mess with Lauren's head or argue with her about religion or logic or ask for favors or anything else.

I just came to say good-bye.

Lauren's cut her hair into bangs that hang out under the home-knit beret-type hat she's got on. A little curtain of blond shields her forehead. The hat's so homely and old-ladyish that it makes me crush on[51] Lauren again so much—even if she did stop praying for me.

It's like she's not even aware that she's so horribly out of fashion. She's not wearing the hat in any ironic way, like some of the black-nail-polish girls in my high school would. And Lauren's also got on this off-white jacket that goes down to her knees and from far away makes her look like she's wearing a robe—like the stereotypical angel a child would draw.

God, she looks perfect.

And no one is paying her any attention but me.

Since I've been watching her, I'd say at least thirty people have passed and she's extended her mitten-clutched pamphlet to every single one and yet no one has even glanced at her.

I still think the idea of god is bullshit, obviously, but I have to tell you, the one thing I admire about Lauren is that she's not out here because she wants to be right or righteous or make people feel bad about what they already believe; she's not really interested in arguing with anyone or anything like that—and I'll admit that maybe subconsciously she needs to prove that her ideas are more important than the ideas of others, but she also really *worries* that everyone is literally going to burn in hell forever and ever and she doesn't want that to happen to anyone at all. It's like she's living in a fairy tale and

---

51 I know it's weird to crush on homely and old-ladyish, but mostly I just like the fact that Lauren looks nothing like the girls in my school. She looks one-of-a-kind pretty. She also looks like she needs to be rescued. Like she's helpless on her own. So pathetic. Maybe the only person more pathetic than me.

she's desperately trying to keep the big bad wolf from devouring us or blowing down our houses. I love her for at least caring about strangers—for at least trying to save people, even if the threat she perceives isn't real.

When I approach her, she doesn't see me at first.

"Excuse me, miss," I say, trying to do Bogart again. "You wouldn't be able to tell me how to make Jesus Christ my Lord and Savior, would you? Because I've been—"

"Stop making fun of me, please, Leonard," she says as five suits pass by her outstretched hand without taking a tract.

"How many people have you saved today?" I ask just to make conversation.

"Why is there no hair hanging down from inside that hat?" she says, which makes me smile, because she noticed I cut it off.

"Got in a fight with some scissors. Have you been praying for me like you said you would?"

"Every day," she says in a way that makes me believe her.

It's depressing, because if she is telling the truth—considering what I'm about to do—it means prayer doesn't work after all.

"You know, I saw this show on TV and it was all about how maybe aliens came to Earth thousands of years ago and gave humans information that we weren't yet ready to fathom— like space travel—and so we maybe made religion out of those ideas, like metaphors to explain what the aliens had told us. Jesus ascending into the heavens. Promising to return again. That sounds like space travel, right?"

"Why are you telling me this?"

"Well, they suggested that prayer was a form of trying to communicate with these aliens. And they said that Indians wore feathers and kings wore crowns as antennas, sort of."

"What are you talking about?"

Just because I want to do something nice before I kill Asher Beal and off myself, I say, "Well, the important thing is that they kept discussing the universality of prayer all over the world and even used scientific instruments to measure the energy that many people praying together creates, suggesting that prayer can be scientifically detected, that it actually changes our surroundings by manipulating electrons or something, and maybe it even helps—regardless of whether we're really communicating with someone, be it a god or aliens or even if we are just meditating. Praying helps, or at least that's what the show suggested. The power of prayer may be real."

"It *IS* real," she says, and starts to turn red. She really looks pissed off. "God hears all of our prayers. Prayer is very powerful."

"I know. I know," I say, realizing that she has no idea what I'm talking about and, worse yet, she won't allow herself to even consider what I'm saying, because it would ruin the illusions she has to cling to if she is to get through her six mandatory weekly unsuccessful hours of trying to convert subway riders to Christianity.

"Can I ask you a question, Lauren?"

She doesn't answer, but manages to get this mom-looking

woman to take a tract. Lauren says "Jesus loves you" to the woman.

"Forget about all the aliens stuff, okay? What I really want to know before I go and never see you again is this—"

"Where are you going?"

I don't want to tell her that I'm going to kill Asher Beal and myself because it will make her worry about me ending up in hell—which is a real place to her—so I say, "I don't know why I said that. I'm just being stupid, but I wanted to ask you—"

She says "Jesus loves you" to another stranger.

"Do you think that maybe if I were a Christian—like maybe if I were born into a family like yours and was home-schooled and forced to believe that—"

"I'm not forced to believe anything. I believe of my own free will."

"Yeah, yeah, I know. But the point I'm trying to make is that if I were more like you, if I believed in god like you do, do you think that maybe you and I could have dated and maybe gotten married and had babies and lived a happily-ever-after sort of life?"

She looks at me like she's trying to make a decision, and then she says, "You could have that sort of life if you ask God for it. If you give your life to God, He will provide for you in marvelous ways. He promises us that. If He takes care of the sparrows, how much more will He take care of us?"

There are a million arguments I could use against her

right now, because not everyone who believes in god gets to live in suburbia and have first-world problems like Baback says, and if believing in god could really solve all of my problems and make me feel better, I would definitely do that pronto—everyone would, right?

But I'm not really interested in debunking her theology right now. I'm much more interested in the fact that Lauren's never been kissed and that I might die without kissing her.

"Just pretend I'm a Christian like you. For argument's sake. Theoretically. Could we have ended up married and living a regular life? Like maybe in an alternate universe?"

"Why are you asking me this?"

She looks really confused and like she might actually run away from me, so I drop it and say, "I bought you a present," and start to open my backpack.

"Why did you buy me a present?"

"This may seem weird, but I feel like god told me to buy you this present." I'm completely lying, but I manage to say it with a serious old-school Hollywood face and I can tell she buys it, mostly because she *wants* to buy it. "He spoke to me. Told me you had been praying hard. And so he wanted me to give you a sign today."

Her lips are parted just a little. She doesn't wear any makeup ever, so she looks natural right now, which I love.

Her breath is slipping in and out of her like a soul yo-yo.

I hand her the little pink box.

"I don't know that I can accept a present from you, Leonard," she says, but she's also staring at the box like she really wants to know what's inside.

"It's from god," I say. "So it's okay."

She sucks her lips in between her teeth and then her mittens come off and she's unwrapping the paper, which makes me so so so happy.

Lauren lifts off the lid and pulls out the silver cross on the silver chain.

"I know how much you love Christianity, so I found this on the Internet. It's simple enough to go with your style, but—"

She clamps it on around her neck, holds the cross in front of her nose, and gives it a good stare before tucking it into her shirt. Then she smiles beautifully.

"Did God really tell you to buy this for me?"

"He sure did," I lie. "I'm really thinking about turning around my life and avoiding hell. Giving my life to Jesus and all the rest. I just have to sort through some issues first, but your dedication, the fact that you stand out here three times a week, the strength of your faith is amazing and really won me over."

Her eyes open wide and I can tell I'm totally making her day, like she was waiting for some sort of signal from god, some sort of affirmation, and I'm her miracle, so I just keep piling it on, talking about being a changed man, and wanting to live a good life, and spending eternity with her in heaven.

Inside I start to feel terrible, thinking about how disappointed she'll be when she sees the news tonight—how crushing that will be for her—and I wonder if her faith will be able to withstand it.

I think god is just a fairy tale, but I'm really starting to like the fact that Lauren has faith.

Don't know why.

It's weird.

A contradiction, maybe.

Or maybe it's like wanting little kids to believe in Santa after someone else already ruined it for you, or you just figured out that your parents were Santa after all and the magic of Christmas instantly evaporated. But thinking about my destroying her faith by tricking her and then killing myself really starts to bring me down, until I just can't lie to her anymore.

"Life can be really hard, you know. It makes it difficult to believe in god sometimes, but I'm trying—for you, and maybe for me too," I say, and then I just start to fucking cry. I'm not sure why. Man, I bawl and bawl.

She hugs me and I clutch her, sob into her neck that smells like vanilla extract baking inside cookies—so fucking wonderful!

The sad suits and briefcases pass us in droves, but no one even seems to notice us as I drink her up.

"God works in mysterious ways," she says, and rubs my back all motherly. "This world is a test. It's hard. But I will continue to pray for you. We could pray together. You could come to church with me. It would help you. My father will help you too."

She's saying all of these really nice things, trying to comfort me the only way she knows how, and I love just being on someone's radar so much that I start kissing her neck and then her mouth. Our tongues touch, and she kisses me back for a fraction of a second—

Her mouth is so warm
and wet and mint-y
from the gum she's
chewing and my
heart's pulsing spikes
of adrenaline through
my veins, which is
exciting and
animalistic and
primal, but maybe not
quite what I was
expecting, because I
thought kissing
Lauren would be like
the epic kisses in
Bogie films, like the
string section would
kick in and I'd get
that swirling feeling

Baback's playing
produces, and Lauren
would pause to gaze
at me and say, "I like
that. I'd like more,"
just like Bacall says—
in that infamous
husky voice—to
Bogie in *The Big
Sleep*, and when I
kissed her glossy
battleship-gray lips
again, she'd say,
"That's even better,"
but instead it's just
the hot sweaty rush of
bodies mangling
when they maybe
shouldn't even be
mingling—and she
tries to push me away,
but the rush forces me
to hold on to her tight,
even though I want to
let go, even though I
should really LET
GO!, so she turns her

face from my mouth
and yells "Stop" in
this high-pitched
squeal that is the
complete antithesis of
Bacall's warm sexy
brassy voice and
when I keep kissing
her cheek and ear, she
smashes my chin with
the heel of her hand,
jolting my brain back
to reality and
knocking off my
Bogart hat in the
process.

I stagger backward and then pick up my fedora.

The warm rush freezes into a heavy lump in my chest and suddenly I feel so so shitty—like I need to vomit.

"Is there a problem here?" says this subway rent-a-cop who has magically appeared. He has this dirt moustache that makes him seem about twelve years old. He's hilarious-looking in his official uniform with the little silver badge. Almost cute. Like a kid wearing a Halloween costume.

"I'm just delivering a message from god," I say, and pop my hat back onto my head. I'm acting again, keeping my true feelings repressed—I'm aware of that, but I can't help it.

Lauren looks at me like maybe I'm a demon from hell or the Antichrist, and says, "Why did you do that?"

"What did you do to her?" the rent-a-cop asks, trying to look official and tough.

"I gave her a cross on a silver chain and tried to tell her I love her—*I do love you, Lauren; I really do*—then I kissed her passionately."

She looks at me with her head all cockeyed and her wet lips parted.

She's so confused.

I'm kind of confused too, because I'm not attracted to Lauren at all anymore and the kiss was a spectacular failure.

I can tell that some part of her deep inside liked the kissing, because it's natural for teenage girls to like kissing, but she feels conflicted, like she's not supposed to like it, that she's supposed to deny her instincts here, like her religious training bids her, and that's what's really eating her up inside.

Maybe that's how rapists justify their actions.

Maybe I'm a monster now.

Because I can see the thought process happening—it's written all over her face.

Yes.

No.

Yes.

No.

Yes.

No.

No.

No.

No.

I can't.

I really can't.

I really truly absolutely can't.

Why did you do this to me?

Why did you make me feel this way?

Why?!?

Lauren says, "I have to go," just before she drops her stack of religious pamphlets and runs away.

I hate myself.

She literally runs.

I really fucking hate myself.

And I don't have the heart to chase, mostly because I used up whatever courage and strength I had just to kiss her.

There's a part of me that still wants to believe the kissing was wonderful.

Black-and-white Bogie-Bacall perfect.

Even though it wasn't.

My dad used to say that the last drink of the day, when the work and thinking are over and you're just about to surrender to unconsciousness, that's always the best drink regardless of how it tastes.

Maybe Lauren was my last drink of the day.

The tracts blow all over the concrete sidewalk like dead leaves in the breeze.

"You better work on your delivery, Romeo," the rent-a-cop says. "Now keep moving."

"Aye, aye," I say, and give the kid a military salute, making my body rigid and stiff, karate-chopping my eyebrows. "Good job keeping people with guns away from the subway. You really are a fantastic rent-a-cop."

He looks at me and puts a hand on this two-foot club strapped to his belt, probably because they won't let the kid carry a gun. He makes this evil twisted face, like beating me to death would really make his day. The rent-a-cop actually intimidates me a little, which is ironic, since I'm going to kill myself. But I haven't shot Asher Beal yet, and death by rent-a-cop is probably even worse than death by übermorons.

"Here's me moving on," I say, and he lets me, because it's the easiest thing for him to do.

He probably makes what—eleven-fifty an hour?

A rent-a-cop's not exactly going to take a bullet in the line of duty for that type of wage, and who would?

As I walk away, my backpack feels lighter.

I've delivered all of my presents, so now it's finally time to kill Asher Beal.

Let's get this birthday party started!

I'm so ready to be done with this life.

It will be so so beautiful to finally be end-of-the-road done.

This will be the best birthday present ever; I'm pretty sure of that.

TWENTY-FOUR

I open my birthday present in the woods behind Asher Beal's house—feel the familiar cold heaviness of the P-38 in my hand—and then wait for my target[52] to come home.

I've been doing reconnaissance for a few weeks now, so I know that on Thursdays my target arrives home around 5:43 from wrestling practice, and then usually goes into his first-floor bedroom for an hour before dinner.

The target usually surfs the Internet while waiting for feeding time, at which point the target will relocate to the kitchen.

The glow of the laptop screen lights up the target's face and makes him look like an alien or a demon or a fish in a lit

---

52 I read on the Internet that the US military employs euphemism to make it easier to kill people. Military men and women shoot "targets," not people, and blow up "targets," not buildings full of women and children. So I employ that little bit of wisdom here. I will shoot a "target" and not a former friend/current classmate. You might think using euphemism is dumb, but you'd be surprised how much it helps to calm the nerves and ease the conscience. It really works.

tank, and watching the target's dead expression illuminated by the screen has also made it easier to visualize killing him—the weird lighting really dehumanizes the target.

I've practiced shooting my target from the tree line, using my hand as a gun.

But today I'm going to creep up to the window, shoot the target through the pane at point-blank range, stick my arm through the jagged glass teeth and pop the target six more times—mixing head shots with chest shots—to ensure the target has been eliminated, and then I'll escape into the woods, where I will off my second target with the last bullet in the magazine before the local cops and maybe even the FBI arrive.

That's my plan.

All I have to do is wait for my target to flick on his bedroom light, which will be the first falling domino to set the chain of events in motion.

TWENTY-FIVE

It's cold and
dark in the
woods and I
wonder if this
is what it's
going to feel
like when I'm
finally dead—
like a stupid
unfeeling
unthinking
unnoticed tree.

I'm hoping to feel nothing.

Übernothing.

I'm hoping that I merely cease to exist.

*What dreams
may come?*

Hamlet and Lauren would ask.[53]

None, I'm betting.

None.

Hellfire is not in the plans.

Heaven is not in the plans.

Cold and dark are not in the plans.

Übernothing.

That's what I want.

Nothing.[54]

---

53 For completely different reasons.

54 "Life's but a walking shadow, a poor player. That struts and frets his hour upon the stage. And then is heard no more: it is a tale told by an idiot—full of sound and fury, signifying nothing." That's William Shakespeare on the type of nothing I DON'T want. I gleaned that little nugget of anti-life-affirming wisdom from last year's English class, when I had to memorize Macbeth's soliloquy. Public school can be a real shot of lithium, let me tell you. It's crazy the pessimistic shit we're made to memorize in school and then carry around in our skulls for the rest of our lives.

TWENTY-SIX

I've been watching the target's mom framed in the kitchen's bay window, the soft overhead light making it look like she's in a film and the bay window is like a drive-in movie screen.

I decide to call the movie *Mrs. Beal Makes Her Perverted Son His Last Meal*.

It's a boring picture in the literal sense, but it conjures up a lot of emotions inside me for personal reasons.

I remember Mrs. Beal being really stupid[55] but sweet on the surface when we were kids.

---

55 Maybe a better word is *oblivious*. She was mentally absent in a way that might be perceived as enlightened or transcendent maybe to the untrained eye, but really she had this disguised sham blind-eye head-in-the-clouds type of defense mechanism at work, which maybe fostered Asher's sense of entitlement and general disregard for the emotional well-being of others—even his best friend at the time. Like one time we were in a T.G.I. Fridays–type restaurant and Asher kept pouring his soda into the huge clay pot of a palm tree close to our table and then raising his glass in the air and demanding endless refills from the waitress, yelling, "More soda!" across the joint. And even though Mrs. Beal must have seen him pouring the soda into the palm tree pot—everyone in the restaurant did, I know because people were shaking their heads by the end of our meal—Asher's mom didn't tell him to knock it off or even

She would always order us a pizza whenever I was over at their house, regardless of whether we were hungry or not. There was always pizza. Pizza was ubiquitous. It's like that was an official rule in their house—when guests under fourteen visit, there shall be pizza, pronto.

She was also always singing songs from the musical *Cats*. So much that I can quote the lyrics of many of the songs, even though I have never seen the show, nor have I ever listened to a recording of the musical.[56]

"Memory" was her favorite.

Although she also liked "Mr. Mistoffelees," who was apparently clever.

It's funny how I'm remembering all of this right now when I'm trying to use military euphemisms, and it makes me sad, because Mrs. Beal has no idea what a Charles Darwin–type favor I'll be doing by killing her son, mostly because she has no idea who her son is—what he has done and of what he's capable.

Not in a million years would she believe what her son made me endure.

---

acknowledge what he was doing in any way at all. She just let him abuse the waitress, who was young and too busy (and maybe too dumb) to argue or do anything but bring Asher endless Cokes. He seemed to delight in abusing the waitress. He smiled and smiled like a boy king, and I hated him on that day even more than I usually hated him back then in junior high. When he turned evil, he really turned evil. It was like something inside him broke and could never be repaired again. He never used to be like that when we were in elementary school, before what happened began and changed everything.
56 Other than what I've heard on elevators.

She wouldn't believe it because if she did, I don't think she'd be able to sing songs from silly musicals while doing housework, and that's her favorite thing to do in the world, or at least it was when I used to hang out with Asher back in middle school.[57]

I try not to think about her hearing the gunshots, her running into Asher's room, her screaming, her maybe even cradling Asher's blood-soaked head in her arms, trying to put his brains back into his skull,[58] and her endless weeping for a fictional boy who didn't ever exist—the son she never had— because she believes her Asher is an absolute angel.

She never saw him change, or if she did, she chose not to believe it, which makes her just as guilty, just as culpable.

I mean, don't get me wrong; I could never shoot Mrs. Beal in the face, because she's always singing songs from *Cats* and never wronged me personally.

But when you really think about it, she's to blame just as much as Linda is—and my dad too, regardless of whether or not he's still alive in Venezuela.

These people we call Mom and Dad, they bring us into the world and then they don't follow through with what we need, or provide any answers at all really—it's a fend-for-yourself free-for-all in the end, and I'm just not cut out for that sort of living.

---

57 It's funny how much I simultaneously like and hate the fact that Mrs. Beal sings, seemingly oblivious to the rest of the world.
58 Which just may mute her singing forever.

Thinking about all of this gets me feeling so low, and I'm shivering now.

"Come on, Target Asher. *Ollie Ollie in come free.* Come home so I can finish this once and for all," I whisper as I watch gray-haired Mrs. Beal pull a small chicken from the oven.

The huge window frames her perfectly as she slices the meat and moves her mouth.

She's singing again.[59]

---

59 This might sound weird, but watching Mrs. Beal sing reminds me of the Dickens *Christmas Carol* display they put up in the city every December. You walk through Victorian England peeping through the windows of miniature houses on fake cobblestone streets lit with gas lamps—and I'm pretty sure the little wooden people sing at some point—as you follow around the three ghosts of Christmas Past, Present, and Future through the life of the miserly miserable Scrooge until he has his change of heart and it's all Merry Christmas and huge-ass turkeys and God bless us every one. My dad took me to Dickens Village once when I was in junior high and therefore too old for such a kid-ish father-son event. He was too high to notice that all the other sons and daughters there were less than four feet tall. He was also too high to notice that he was kind of staggering bleary-eyed and everyone was staring at him. Ironically, my dad was a big fan of Christmas. It always got the bastard feeling sentimental, which forced him to do even more drugs and drink—two of his favorite activities.

TWENTY-SEVEN

There's part of me—deep down inside—that feels the need to make a confession here, especially before I go through with my plan and therefore will not be able to make any sort of statement ever again.

A few months after we went to the Green Day concert, Asher spent the weekend with his uncle Dan fishing somewhere in rural Pennsylvania—I think it might have been the Poconos. He loved his uncle Dan, who was tall and confident and funny and drove a cool truck and was always taking Asher places—like to the movies and car races and even hunting. Uncle Dan seemed like the kind of uncle every kid dreams of having. I remember liking him immediately when we first met. He really seemed like a great guy, which makes it all the worse.[60]

---

60 Why is it that great guys almost always let you down just as soon as you start to believe in them? Is that a rule of the universe or something? WTF?

But when Asher came back from this particular fishing trip—something wasn't right.

We had this project for school we were working on—about ancient civilizations—and we had picked the Incas. We were putting the finishing touches on a miniature Machu Picchu at his house the Sunday night after he returned from fishing with Uncle Dan. I remember Asher wouldn't look me in the eye and kept saying "Nothing!" way too loud every time I asked if anything was wrong. Finally he said, "If you ask me what's wrong one more time, I'm going to beat the shit out of you." He stared at me—like he wanted to kill me and was capable of doing it too.

I didn't say anything as we finished creating our Machu Picchu. We had built the skeleton out of LEGOs, had used real sod for the grass, and had been making little cube-shaped papier-mâché buildings for weeks. In my memory, the project looks magnificent—like I'd never made something so beautiful before or since. And Asher had been really proud of it just the week before—excited even. But just as I put the final bit of paint on the last structure, Asher started to smash the project with his fists.

"What are you doing?" I yelled, because we had spent *weeks* on it.

He just kept punching and smashing, sending down fists from above like some cruel boy-god.

It was so fucking awful to watch—not just because he

180

was ruining all of our hard work, but because I could clearly see he was coming undone.

I tried to grab him and he punched me in the face hard—giving me a black eye.

Then he just started to cry in this really violent way.

His mother came in and saw what was going on. She said, "What happened?"

I stood there with my mouth open as she tried to hug Asher, but he just ran right by her and into his room.

I'd never been so confused.

I couldn't even explain what had happened to my parents, because I had no idea.

You'd think they would have called Mrs. Beal and asked a bunch of questions, but I don't think they did, and I remember my dad saying, "Boys fight at that age. Just part of growing up," to Linda, who was more concerned with how ugly my black eye appeared than the reason for Asher's freak-out.

Asher didn't come to school for a few days, and then he just showed up at my house late one afternoon and said, "Can we talk?"

"Sure," I said.

My dad and Linda weren't home. We went up into my room and he started pacing like a caged animal. I had never seen him pace like that before.

"I'm sorry I fucked up our project," he said.

"It's okay." I didn't really care about failing or anything

like that, but what he had done to me definitely wasn't okay, and I knew it.

Why did I say it was okay?

I should have said, "Why the hell did you punch me? What the fuck is wrong with you?" But I didn't.

I wish I had.

Maybe if I had gotten angry…

"Something happened on the fishing trip," he said.

He looked at me in this crazy way.

He looked so desperate.

But then he broke eye contact, said, "Never mind. I have to go," and walked out of my room.

I was so confused that I let him walk away without saying a word. I know now that I should have chased him, asked again what was wrong, promised to help him, or—at the very least—I should have told someone that Asher was acting weird, but I was afraid of that desperate look. I didn't want Asher to punch me again—and I was just a kid.

How was I supposed to know what to do?

The next day, Asher returned to school and really appeared to be okay. For a while everything seemed to go back to normal. Our teacher even let us redo our Machu Picchu model for three-quarters credit, which we accomplished in half the time it took us to build the original.

But then Asher started picking fights with kids at school who were small and quiet.

He started to make fun of me during lunch periods—

saying crazy weird stuff like he caught me jerking off to a picture of his mom, or that I tried to grab his dick in the locker room—and he was always trying to trip me in the halls and pushing me into lockers.

I didn't like it at all, but I didn't say anything.

Why?

I should have said something—not just to stick up for myself, but because I think Asher wanted me to save him.

Like maybe he wanted me to make it stop the whole time and on some subconscious level he was pushing me to get so fucking angry that I would finally tell the adults in our lives that he needed help. I wonder now if all of what happened afterward—the bullying and then the really bad shit—was his way of punishing me for failing to protect him.

When I finally stood up for myself—when he stopped with me—I knew there would be others.

What if I had the power to save both of us—*all of us*—all along?

I need to take care of what I should have taken care of a long time ago.

I need to make it stop permanently.

TWENTY-EIGHT

My target suddenly makes an appearance in *Mrs. Beal Makes Her Perverted Son His Last Meal*—there he is on the kitchen's bay-window drive-in movie screen.

I start to sweat.

Enemy collateral target known as "Asher's mother" gives the primary target a kiss on the cheek.

Primary target says something before disappearing.

Primary target looks like the all-American next-door boy in the movie—like the kid you'd pick to take your daughter to the prom. The dutiful-son lie plastered all over that drive-in movie screen gets my heart pumping machine-gun blood drops that race through my veins as I turn the P-38 safety off with my thumb and finger the trigger.[61]

Every inch of my skin is slick with sweat, even though it's

---

61 The trigger reminds me of a frozen snake's tongue.

probably less than forty degrees out. A minute ago I was shivering, but now I fight an urge to take off my shirt—that's how hot I feel. It's like I swallowed the sun.

Primary target's bedroom light comes on a second later, which is supposed to be my cue to move and put the plan into action, but my feet remain rooted to the ground.

Primary target flicks on his computer and his face glows like an alien.

Kill the alien, I think.

Remember what he did to you.

You have every right.

He's not human.

He's a thing.

A target.

Remember to use your military training—what you gleaned from the Internet.

I leave my body and my essence floats up maybe fifteen feet above my head so that I am looking down on the flesh and bones and blood—the matter—I used to inhabit.

I can't see my expression because of the Bogart hat, but my right arm is outstretched and the P-38 is pointed at the primary target.

My legs don't walk, but I start to glide across the backyard, through the darkness, light as a ghost.

I look like a rigid lowercase *r* being pulled across ice.

What's pulling me? I think as I hover through the stiff

winter air looking down, which is when I realize my essence is being pulled too—I'm sort of following my flesh like a helium birthday balloon tied to a little kid's wrist.[62]

I'm standing in the target's window now, remembering what he did to me in that very bedroom so many times.

How confused I felt.

How I wanted it to stop.

How he intimidated me.

How he psychologically tricked me.

How he said if I stopped doing what we were doing he'd tell people in great detail all about what we had done together and then everyone would call me a faggot and maybe even beat the shit out of me.

People would believe him and not me, when he said *I* made *him* do it.

And how if I stopped doing what he wanted me to do he'd post the video he secretly made of us with his computer camera that I didn't know was on.

The first time, he said his uncle had shown him how to feel good in a way I wouldn't believe.

I wanted to feel good.

Who doesn't?

We were almost twelve.

---

62 This is what used to happen when I was alone with Asher in his bedroom too—I'd just sort of detach and float above as what happened happened. And for a while that was enough to protect me from feeling too bad. It was like what was happening was happening to someone else, while I floated safely with my back against the ceiling and my eyes closed.

We were wrestling WWE-style.

Just messing around.

I had this ski mask I'd wear and pretend I was Rey Mysterio.

He was always John Cena.

And then we weren't wrestling.

We were doing something I didn't understand—something exciting, dangerous.

Something I wasn't ready for—something I didn't really want.

We were pretending—or were we?

Then Asher wanted to wrestle all the time.

I started asking questions—trying to figure out what was happening.

Asher told me not to ask questions—to keep what happened between us, not to think about it too much—and he looked mean when he said it, like someone I didn't know, not like a friend at all.

The more it happened, the less friendly he got.

It went on for two years.

I didn't want to lose my friend.

Haven't you ever done things you didn't want to do just to keep a friend?

I tried to avoid Asher's bedroom—being alone with Asher period—but he was persistent, always asking me to wrestle, which became the code word.

Then I just started making up excuses—telling Asher I

couldn't hang out because I had homework, or my mom had grounded me, or whatever. He got the hint quick, which is when he started to threaten me.

It ended with a fistfight—Asher beating the shit out of me because I refused to "keep wrestling."

He was always stronger, bigger.

I didn't care about the beating.

And my not caring freed me.

When I made it clear that he'd have to give me regular black eyes—wounds that would get people asking a lot of questions—to keep it going, that's when it stopped.

Maybe that's when I became a man.

When my parents asked about the bruises, I told them Asher and I had another fight.

They didn't ask any follow-up questions.

Maybe because they suspected I was gay.

I think I tried to tell Linda once, but she refused to believe it and changed the subject. I don't remember exactly what I said, but I was probably indirect, because how can you be direct about shit like that when you're just going through puberty? Sometimes I remember her laughing, like I had told a joke. Sometimes I remember laughing too, just because it felt safer to laugh, although maybe I made that part up. The memory of that attempt to communicate is all fucking blurry, so I don't really know.

No one ever found out the truth and that seems wrong—dangerous even.

188

I became a freak, while Asher somehow went on to become popular and well-adjusted and what most people would call normal, at least on the outside.

The bullies are always popular.

Why?

People love power.

Will I become temporarily powerful if I shoot Asher?[63] I've been wondering.

But—standing there outside his window—I become that scared little kid again whose parents are oblivious and gone; whose mother doesn't even say a word when she walks in on her son and his best friend naked one day, but simply shuts the door and pretends it never happened.[64]

But for some reason—regardless of all that—I start thinking about this one summer day, before all of the weirdness started, back when we were just two kids.

It's the last good memory I have of my old friend.

For no reason at all, Asher and I decided to ride our bikes as far as we could before we were due home for dinner.

We left at nine AM and had to return by five PM.

That gave us eight hours, so we decided to ride in one direction for three and a half hours, and then simply turn

---

63 The news world will make me instantly famous for sure, and what is fame if it isn't power and popularity?

64 I remember that happening suddenly. I do. It's a real memory. Where did it come from?

around and ride home for four and a half, figuring we'd be tired on the return trip, so it would take longer.

It was a pointless thing to do—the type of plan kids come up with when they are bored to death in the summer. But we had never really left our town before without our parents, we knew we definitely weren't allowed to do this, and so our hearts pounded as we began pedaling defiantly. It felt like we were embarking on an amazing, forbidden adventure.

I remember Asher leading the way through all of these towns we'd never been to before even though they were close by and I remember experiencing a sense of freedom that was new and alive and intoxicating.

I remember being forced to stop when a red-and-white gate came down, and as we watched a train pass, I noticed Asher's T-shirt was soaked in sweat. He had us pedaling hard and my thighs were on fire for most of the trip, but they burned hottest then, when we were forced to wait idle.

When the train passed and the gate went up, we were off again.

He kept looking back over his shoulder and smiling at me—and I loved him in the sort of way you love a brother or a trusted friend—even as the bugs kept hitting my face and the summer wind blew back my hair.

I remember sitting by a pond in a formerly unknown-to-us park located in a town where we knew no one—eating the slices of leftover pizza we had wrapped in tinfoil and stuffed into our backpacks.

We didn't even really say anything to each other, but smiled because we were rebelling—out in the great big world on our own—and we couldn't believe how easy it was, how you could hop on your bike, pedal, and disappear from under your parents' thumbs, from everything you knew, and how there was so much out there for us to explore.

That day buzzed with possibility.

We both felt it, and so there was no need to put it into words.

Everything was understood.

What happened to us?

What happened to those two kids who simply loved to ride bikes for hours and hours?

The mouth of my P-38 is almost touching the glass now.

Primary target doesn't sense I'm just outside his window.

Primary target is approximately five feet away.

If your grandfather could execute an evil man, so can you, I think.

The computer screen casts an eerie glow over the target's bedroom.

As I hover above my body, I try to move my index finger so that it will trip the trigger

and the

P-38

will
dischar
ge and
the
glass
will
shatter
and the
target's
head
will
explod
e like a
pumpk
in.

But that doesn't happen for some reason.

The target clicks off his computer and the room goes dark.

It takes a few seconds for my eyes to adjust, but when they do I see that Asher has his dick in his hand and he's jerking off in his chair, only he's turned sideways so that his pumping fist won't bang the underbelly of his desk. He's even thrown back his head.

But, amazingly, even with Asher jerking off five feet away, I just can't stop thinking about that day we went for that long-ass bike ride and wishing we could erase everything that happened since and live in the space of that one single day.

I remember turning around at the designated time so we wouldn't be late for dinner, so we wouldn't arouse our parents' suspicions.

We were in front of a car dealership and there were all of these red, white, and blue balloons left over from the Fourth of July. We put our feet on the concrete, straddled our bikes, and surveyed the new land we'd discovered.

It was like we were little Christopher Columbuses or Ponce de Leóns.

Like we had left safe land and survived unknown waters.

BMX bikes were our ships.

Asher said, "We made it pretty far."

I nodded and smiled.

"We can do this every day this summer. Go in so many different directions! Like the spokes of our bike wheels!"

I remember the look on his face was genuine pure excitement—like we had just discovered we had wings and could fly.

His eyes radiated like the summer sun above us.

But we never did go on another bike ride like that ever again, and I'll never understand why.

Our parents didn't catch us.

We didn't get into any trouble at all.

The trip was a complete success.

We just never got around to taking another daylong ride, maybe because of what Asher's uncle started, and that seems so so fucking sad right now, such a missed opportunity, that my eyes get all watery and my vision blurs.

My P-38 is
still pointed
at the primary
target, but I'm
starting to realize
that I'm not
going to
complete
this mission.
I'm
a
terrible
soldier.

My grandfather would probably call me a faggot and slap the shit out of me, like he used to do to my father, or so my mother told me at my grandfather's funeral, when I was in the third grade.

My heart's just not in it, but I'm not really sure why.

Probably because I'm a fuckup who can't do anything right.

My essence gets sucked back into my body and then I'm clicking the P-38 safety back on.

I stuff the gun into my front pocket, pull out my cell phone, and hit the power button.

As soon as it loads up I tap the camera icon, make sure the flash is on, point it at Asher's bedroom window, discharge an explosion of white light so he will know someone has taken a picture of him jerking off, and then run like hell through the woods.

TWENTY-NINE

As I snake through so many leafless trees, kicking through mounds of dead foliage and fallen branches, I keep tripping and worrying about the P-38 accidentally firing a bullet into my thigh—but I keep laughing too.

I picture Asher jumping up when he saw the flash and then scurrying to the window and seeing someone running for the woods.

I wonder if he knew it was me.

Of course he knew it was me!

Who else would it be?

Although he probably has many enemies and maybe even has a new secret boy, now that I'm out of the picture.

Still, whether he knows it was me or not, he's probably worried about that photo showing up on Facebook or being posted all over the hallways of our school—and even though

I would never do either of those things,[65] it's still kind of funny thinking about Asher's jerk-off picture going public.

I mean, think of the meanest person you know.

Think of Hitler, even.

And then picture him jerking off alone in a room.

Suddenly, he doesn't seem so evil and impressive anymore, does he?

He seems sort of hilarious and powerless and vulnerable and maybe even like someone you feel sorry for.

Back in junior high, our health teacher told us that everyone masturbates.

Everyone is a slave to sexual desire, I guess.

And so maybe everyone deserves our pity, then, too.

Maybe if we would just picture our enemies jerking off once in a while, the world would be a better place.

I don't know.

Somehow I end up by the river and decide to catch my breath under this little bridge where there are endless empty beer cans, shards of cheap alcohol bottles that were long ago thrown against the massive concrete wall, used condoms here

---

65 Mostly because I'd be too afraid of what people would say about me if they deduced just who it was that took the photo and then, therefore, would know I was watching Asher through his bedroom window. "Why?" they'd ask me. Explaining the reason to übermorons would be worse than death any day. And Asher would definitely incriminate me if that picture ever got out. He'd drag me down with him for sure. Offer me up to the übermorons like a sacrifice. They'd believe whatever he said too, because he's more like them than I am.

and there, and all sorts of graffiti—gems like "Rich fucked Neda here 10-3-09" and "Super Cock Hero!" and "Tru Nigga 4 life," even though there are no black people living in our town.

Kids in my high school drink beer under this bridge, and call it Troll City, although I've never been to any of those parties.

As I catch my breath, I think about Asher and laugh once more.

What he did to me doesn't seem all that important anymore, because I'm about to blow my brains out, and so the memory of it will instantly disappear and be gone forever.

End of problem.

And I tell myself that he's freaked out about the photo I took—that will have to be his punishment.

I've evened the score.

I can let go.

I can finally close my eyes and fall backward into the deep beyond.

I try to believe that anyway.

For some crazy reason, I remember this quote about living with what you've done and that being a significant punishment of its own. Herr Silverman had us debate this quote in Holocaust class when we were talking about the Jews who searched the globe hunting for escaped Nazis after WWII—men who had done evil, horrible things and then fled to Argentina or Namibia or wherever.

A lot of kids in my class argued the validity of that quote, probably because they thought taking the high road was the right answer, what Herr Silverman wanted, the response that would score you the most points on the SAT.

I know Herr Silverman wasn't saying the Nazis who fled should be forgiven and given a fresh start. He was trying to make us think about how life is hard and people suffer in all sorts of ways without our adding to their suffering to satisfy our sense of vengeance, but I sort of don't think that the quote holds up in the real world, where literature and schooling and philosophy and morality don't exist, because Asher and Linda and so many other culpable people seem to be fine—functioning exceptionally well within the world even—while I'm under a disgusting bridge about to put a hole in my skull.

Maybe this is how the Jewish Nazi hunters felt back in the fifties—like they were still living in Troll City even after they had been liberated from the Nazi death camps.

Or maybe this is justice.

Maybe I've allowed myself to become this fucked-up, depressed, misunderstood person.

Maybe this is all my fault.

Maybe I should have killed Asher Beal.

I mean, I was so angry.

Asher definitely deserved to die.[66]

---

[66] It makes me think about how Hamlet had the chance to kill Claudius while he was praying, but didn't since Claudius had just made peace with god, asked for god's forgiveness, and therefore was eligible for entrance into heaven, as Lauren will tell you. So Hamlet waited for a time when Claudius was sinning. Would Hamlet have

Or maybe I should have tried to save Asher back when all the bad shit began—before he turned full-on evil?

But I was just a kid.

We were just kids, and maybe we still are.

You can't expect kids to save themselves, can you?

I've got the gun to my temple now and I'm rubbing the side of my head into the metal O.

It feels sort of nice—almost like a massage—as I push the P-38's mouth harder and deeper into the soft spot of my skull.

It's like the P-38 is an old skeleton key I'm trying to fit into an old padlock and when I make that connection I'll hear a click and a door will open and I'll walk through and be saved.

"Make that lock click, Leonard," I whisper to myself. "You just have to squeeze your index finger and everything will be okay. The thoughts will stop. No more problems. You can finally just rest."

I'm just about to pull the trigger when another random question pops into my head.

I wonder whether Linda ever remembered that it was my birthday.

For some reason it seems important right now and the more I wonder the more I realize I just can't die without knowing the answer.

---

killed Claudius if he had found him jerking off like Asher? For some reason, I don't think so, which makes me feel better. Who could kill someone while they were jerking off? It seems impossible. I bet Hamlet would have laughed if he found his father's murderer rubbing one out. *How could you not laugh?*

I lower the P-38 and check my phone for voice messages.
There are none.
I check my e-mail.
Nothing.
Nor are there any text messages.
I laugh—I mean I fucking howl, because it seems so fitting somehow.
What a birthday it's been.
What a life.
I raise the P-38 and press the mouth into my temple once more.
I close my eyes.
I squeeze the trigger.

THIRTY

Time

comes

to

a

standstill.

THIRTY-ONE

The trigger resists and I wonder if it might be rusted or something, because no matter how hard I squeeze, the bullet doesn't come out and I do not die.

So I transfer the gun into my left hand and try to straighten my trigger finger and find that I can't—it's sort of frozen in a cat's curled-tail position that I cannot alter.

"FUCK!!!" I scream into the night, across the water, and then bang my fist against the concrete wall, trying to get my trigger finger to work, but no matter what I do, no matter how hard I try, I just can't seem to blow my brains out.

I wonder if my inability is some sort of subconscious attempt to save myself from suicide and then I remember that I promised to at least call Herr Silverman if I was about to end my life, so I figure I maybe have to make good on that promise before my subconscious will allow me to employ my trigger finger and finish the job.

A promise is a promise.

I find the piece of paper Herr Silverman gave me; it's in my back pocket.

I use my cell phone as a flashlight so I can read the green numbers.

I punch in the numbers.

The phone rings.

I wonder if he will pick up and I'm sort of hoping for voice mail so that I can just leave a message—keeping my promise—and then finish what I've set in motion.

On the fourth ring I relax, thinking I'm about to get his voice mail, when I hear a click and then, "Hello?"

Suddenly it feels like my mouth has jumped off my face, abandoning me, so I couldn't speak even if I wanted to.

"Hello?" Herr Silverman says.

It's definitely his voice.

I attempt to throw my cell phone into the river, but it seems to have become a part of my ear.

"Hello?" Herr Silverman says, a little more forcefully this time.

I'm waiting for him to hang up, thinking it's a wrong number or a perverted heavy breather.

"*Is this Leonard?*" Herr Silverman says in this softer voice, and he doesn't sound like he's pissed that I called. It almost sounds like he's honored. Like he could have said, "*Did I really win teacher of the year?*" in the same voice.

Still, I can't speak.

"Are you okay?" When I don't answer, he says, "Leonard,

don't hang up. Stay on the line. I want to tell you why I don't roll up my sleeves, like I promised. Since you're calling me at this number, I assume that you need to know the answer. I'm happy to tell you. But the problem is that I need to *show* you. So where are you? Tell me and I'll come to you. But I want to keep you on the line while I take a cab. We can chat about anything you want and then when I arrive at wherever you are, I'll roll up my sleeves and explain the mystery to you. I really think you'll find my story worthwhile if you can just hold on until I get there. Can you do that? *Can you do that for me?*"

I don't say anything, although I want to.

My mouth is still missing.

I wasn't expecting this.

I wonder why Herr Silverman is being so nice to me—if he's done this sort of thing with other students. It doesn't seem right to make him come out on a school night when he probably has a million other things to do and therefore doesn't really need this sort of extra above-and-beyond hassle. It would be easier for everyone if I just pulled the trigger and ended this now. But I can't for some reason. I just can't.

"Okay, Leonard. Just make a noise if it's really you. Just grunt or something to let me know. Let's start there. So is it you?"

Even though I tell myself to remain quiet, that I shouldn't be putting Herr Silverman out, that I should just hang up before this gets any more complicated, an "Um-hmmm" rises up from somewhere inside me and makes my lips vibrate.

I'm shaking now, really hard.

"Are you at home?"

I don't say anything.

"Okay, you're not at your house. So where are you?"

I don't say anything.

"Are you alone?"

I don't say anything.

"Just tell me where you are, Leonard. I'll come to you. We can talk. I'll tell you my secret. I'll roll up my sleeves for you."

I don't know why I can suddenly speak, but even though I want to hang up and let Herr Silverman enjoy his night, my lungs and tongue and lips betray me.

"It's my birthday today. No one remembered."

It sounds so stupid and pathetic and little-kid whiny that I push the P-38's barrel into my temple again.

End this.

Just pull the trigger.

Make it easier for everyone.

There's a long pause, and I can tell that Herr Silverman is trying to decide what to say.

"Happy birthday, Leonard. *Are you eighteen today?*"

Hearing someone say "happy birthday"—I know it seems so fucking stupid, but it sort of makes me feel better all of a sudden.

Just two words.

Happy birthday.

It makes me feel like I'm not already gone.

Like I'm still here.

"*Leonard?*" Herr Silverman says.

I'm sort of staring out across the river at the Philadelphia skyline in the distance. The lights of the skyscrapers shimmy across the water and dance with moonbeams.

I wonder if it's anyone else's birthday in Philadelphia.

How those other people are celebrating.

If any of them feel the way I do right now.

"Leonard, please. Just tell me where you are. I'll come to you."

I can't believe how much I want to see Herr Silverman right now.

I don't even really understand why.

I lower the P-38 and tell him where I am.

"Don't move," Herr Silverman says. "I'll be there in twenty minutes. And don't hang up. I'm going to stay on the phone with you. I just have to tell my roommate where I'm going."

I hear him talking to someone, but I don't catch exactly what's being said.

Another man says something in response—it sounds like they are arguing—then there's a rustling noise, and Herr Silverman says, "You still there, Leonard?"

"Yeah."

"I'm walking down the stairs in my apartment building, getting closer to you. Okay, now I'm on Walnut Street looking for a cab. Here's one now. I've got my hand in the air. He sees me. He's pulling over. I'm getting into the cab." I hear him tell the driver where I am. "We're driving now, headed for the bridge."

Herr Silverman narrates his whole trip for me like that and I listen to the sound of his voice and think that his words are the only thing keeping me tethered to this world right now—that his words are literally keeping me alive—and if he hadn't picked up I really might have blown my brains out.

I'm wondering again what might be under his shirtsleeves— if knowing will be worth sticking around.

Or will it be just another in a long list of disappointments?

You still have the gun. You can still check out if you need to, fall into the water, sink … sink … sink into oblivion, I tell myself, and that also helps, because it means I have options.

Options are important.

So is an exit plan.

"Okay," Herr Silverman says, "I'm in New Jersey. About five minutes away from you now."

The lights reflected on the river look so beautiful, I think. They almost make me want to go swimming.

"I can see the bridge now," Herr Silverman says, and then I hear him ask the taxi driver to leave the meter running and wait for us.

The taxi driver says something and the tone of his voice makes me think he won't wait.

"This is serious—*an emergency*," Herr Silverman tells him. "I will tip you well. I promise."

I realize that Herr Silverman is willing to spend his own money to save me[67] and my throat constricts as I hear the taxi come to a stop above me on the bridge.

"I'm leaving the taxi, Leonard. I'm here. I just have to find a way down to you."

I want to tell him there's a little dirt path worn into the hill by drunken high school students, but my mouth has jumped off my face again.

"Here's a path," Herr Silverman says, and then I hear rocks and loose dirt rolling down the hill.

"Leonard?" he says, only this time he's not in my phone.

I hang up.

---

67 And given what public school teachers are paid, this is really saying something.

THIRTY-TWO

"Is that a gun in your hand, Leonard?" Herr Silverman says, and his voice sounds a little shakier than usual—like maybe he's more freaked than he's letting on.

"Nazi P-38," I say, and my voice sounds hard.

"Your grandfather's war trophy?"

I nod.

He's still a few feet away from me, but I feel sort of boxed in a little, so I take a step back.

"You wanna give that to me?" he says, and takes a step toward me with his palm outstretched. I can tell he's really freaked now, because his hand is shaking, although he's trying hard to steady it.

"Did they teach you how to deal with an armed student when you attended teacher school?" I say, trying to lighten the mood. "Was there a class on this?"

"No, they certainly didn't—and there definitely wasn't," he says. "Maybe there should have been. *Is it loaded?*"

"Yep. And the safety's off," I say, hearing the edge in my voice.

Herr Silverman lowers his hand and stiffens a bit.

I don't really understand why I'm speaking to Herr Silverman this way.

I mean—he came to save me, right?

I called him on the phone because I wanted him to come.

But it's like I can't help myself.

It's like I'm too fucked up to be nice and appreciative.

"Just give me the gun and everything will be okay."

"No it won't. That's such a fucking lie! You don't lie, Herr Silverman. You're better than the rest. You're the only adult I really trust and look up to. So tell me something else, okay? Try again."

"Okay. Did you write the letters from the people in the future?" Herr Silverman asks.

His asking that kind of surprises me, and invokes all these intense feelings I don't want to feel. "Yes. Yes, I did," I say in this defiant, almost yelling voice.

"What did they tell you? What did they say?"

"They said a nuclear holocaust is coming. The future world is covered with water, like Al Gore predicted. People kill each other for the little land left. Millions die."

"Interesting. But I'm sure they said other things too, because you're not all gloom and doom, Leonard. I've seen the light in your eyes too many times. What else did they say?"

His saying that bit about there being light in my eyes makes my throat constrict even more and my eyes start to feel tight. "It doesn't fucking matter, because those people don't exist."

"Yes, they do, Leonard," he says, taking another cautious step toward me. "They really do. If you believe hard enough—and if you hold on. Okay—maybe you won't find those exact people, but friends will arrive at some point. You'll find others like you."

"How do you know? How can you be so sure?"

"Because I used to write letters to myself from the future when I was your age and it helped me a great deal."

"But did you meet the people you imagined in the future?"

"I did."

I'm kind of caught off guard by this information, and suddenly I'm truly curious about Herr Silverman's life.

Who are the people he wrote to?

"How did you find them?"

"Writing those letters helped me figure out who I was and what I wanted. Once I knew that, I could send out a clear message so that others could respond appropriately."

I think about it and say, "In the future I man a lighthouse with my wife, daughter, and father-in-law. We send out a great beam of light every night even though no one ever sees it."

"That's beautiful," he says. "You see?"

But I don't see, so I say, "Writing those letters made me feel even more fucked up."

"Why?"

"I got to thinking that I wanted to live in that fictional

217

world *now*—that the better world in the letters made me want to exit this world. That's probably what led to me being here with a gun in my hand."

Herr Silverman winces almost unnoticeably, but I see it. Then he says, "You ever feel like you're sending out a light but no one sees it?"

I look at the lights of the skyline reflected in the water and think about how they are always here—every night—whether people look or not.

And mostly, people don't look.

It doesn't matter what I do.

It really doesn't.

Herr Silverman steps closer, and I don't back away. He takes off his coat, puts it between his knees, and starts to roll up his right sleeve, which makes my heart pound again, because I've wanted to know what the hell is under his sleeves for so long now.

When he gets the cuff up around his elbow, he uses his cell phone to light his wrist. "Take a look."

I don't see scars or needle marks or an abundance of hair or an unsightly burn or anything like that.

It's a tattoo of a pink triangle—what the Nazis used to label homosexuals in the concentration camps; I know because Herr Silverman taught us that.

"Who did that to you?" I ask, thinking that maybe he had his own version of Asher Beal.

"I did it to myself. Well, I hired a tattoo artist to do it."

"Oh," I say.

It takes a moment, but finally, I realize what he's telling me.

"I don't care that you're gay. It doesn't bother me," I say, because I feel like I should.

I never really thought about Herr Silverman being gay before, but it sort of makes sense in retrospect. He never wore a wedding ring, nor did he ever talk about his wife—and he's a good-looking, well-dressed, middle-aged, steadily employed man who would make someone a great husband.

He smiles at me. "Thanks."

"Why did you tattoo your wrist like that?"

"I tried to be who I thought the world wanted me to be all through high school. Always trying to please everyone else—keeping my true self invisible. It took me nineteen years to figure out who I was and another twelve or so months to admit it. I didn't want to ever forget again. I tattooed my wrist with a symbol. So the answer would always be there."

"Why *that* symbol?" I say.

"I think you know why, Leonard. It's probably the same reason you have a Nazi gun in your hand. I was trying to prove something to myself. I was trying to take control."

"So why don't you show your students your tattoo?"

"Because it might hinder my ability to get an important message to people who need it."

"What's the message?"

"It's the message of my classes—especially my Holocaust class."

"Yeah, but what is it?"

"What do you think it is?"

"That it's okay to be different? We should be tolerant."

"That's part of it."

"So why not be different and promote tolerance by showing everyone your pink triangle?"

"Because that might make it difficult for some of your classmates to take me and my message seriously. It's sort of don't ask, don't tell for gay high school teachers—especially those of us who teach controversial Holocaust classes," Herr Silverman says, and then starts rolling up his other sleeve almost all the way to his armpit. "Here—use my phone to read this."

I transfer the P-38 to my left hand and take hold of his cell phone.

I run the light up the inside of his entire arm.

First they ignore you, then they laugh at you, then they fight you, then you win.

The words are printed in navy blue—just simple block letters stacked in two rows. Nothing like the fancy-word tattoos you see sprawled in cursive or Old English across the chests of rappers and famous movie stars. I get the sense that this tattoo is more about the message than the image—the message to himself and no one else, which is probably one of the reasons he keeps it hidden under his shirtsleeve.

"It's often attributed to Gandhi," he says. "But I didn't care who said it when I came across it. I only knew that it made me feel strong. Gave me hope. Kept me going."

"But why did you tattoo that up your arm?"

"So I wouldn't forget that I win in the end."

"How do you know you win?"

"Because I keep fighting."

I think about what he means, about the message he sends out every day in the classroom, why he's telling me this, and say, "I'm not like you."

"Why do you have to be like me? You should be like *you*."

I raise the P-38 to my head and say, "This is me. Right here. Right now."

"No, it's not you at all."

"How would you even know?"

"Because I've read your essays. And I've looked into your eyes when I lecture. I can tell you get it—you're different. And I know how hard being different can be. But I also know how powerful a weapon being different can be. How the world needs such weapons. Gandhi was different. All great people are. And unique people such as you and me need to seek out other unique people who understand—so we don't get too lonely and end up where you did tonight."

"I'm not gay," I say.

"You don't have to be gay to be different. I never thought you were gay."

"I'm really not gay."

"Okay."

"I'm not gay."

"Fine."

"I'm not gay."

"Why are you saying that over and over?"

"Asher Beal is gay."

"Why are you telling me that?"

"He's not gay like you. He's horrible."

"What are you trying to tell me, Leonard?"

"I went to Asher Beal's house tonight. I was going to kill him. I really was. I've wanted to kill him for a long time now."[68]

Herr Silverman gets this horrible panicked look on his face. "But you *didn't* kill him, right?"

"I walked up to his bedroom window with the gun in my hand. I raised the P-38 up to the window, aimed at his head— but I couldn't do it. I just couldn't."

"That's a *good* thing."

"I *should* have killed him."

"What did he do to you?"

I don't want to tell Herr Silverman, and so we stand there in silence for a long time.

But he's patient—he just waits like he's not going to move

---

68 It sounds so weird to be saying the word *kill* to my Holocaust teacher—admitting that I actually attempted to kill a classmate. Allowing the words to exist in the two or so feet between Herr Silverman and me—it feels surreal. It makes me realize how crazy I was earlier—how crazy I've been. I'm simultaneously freaked out and relieved. Fucked but freed, if that makes any sense at all. Reminds me of what Herr Silverman says about doubling in his Holocaust class.

or talk for a million years if that's how long it takes me to answer his question. I don't know why, but his waiting like that makes me feel safe—like I can trust him, like maybe he really, truly believes I'm worth listening to, worth saving. Finally, my mouth rebels against my mind, and all the words come out in a rush—like I'm trying to purge.

I tell him everything.

                                                    Every.
                                   Horrible.
                          Stomach-wrenching.
                   Detail.

                                          And
                                          I'm
                                                         fuckin
                                          g
                                          crying
                                                         again
                                          because
                                                         I
                                          just
                                                         can't
                                          help
                                                         it.

At some point, while I'm losing it, Herr Silverman puts his arm around me and starts to pat my back. He's really careful about it—cautious—but I can tell that he's only trying to comfort me. It feels right. Safe. And so I let him hug me, and

223

it feels okay to be hugged, even though I don't hug him back, which probably makes him feel awkward, and I feel sorry about that, but I'm just not a natural hugger when I get upset like this. He keeps whispering, "You're okay," and I simultaneously love him and hate him for saying that. I'm fucking not okay at all. And yet it's exactly what I most want to be: okay. He can't give that to me, but I love him for trying.

I wonder if Herr Silverman thinks he has the power to make lies into truths just by repeating words over and over—like a magic spell.

There's part of me that hopes he does.

There's also part of me that wants to scream FUCK YOU! in his face.

Those two opposites battle inside my rib cage for a long time.

Finally, I calm down and he lets go and we both look out over the water without saying anything—just breathing.

It feels like hours go by, but I like standing there with Herr Silverman at my side.

I feel empty.

Thoroughly purged.

And for a second or two I pretend that we are manning Lighthouse 1—together.

Herr Silverman finally says, "You know that men can be raped, right?"

I don't say anything, but I wonder if that's what happened to me because I didn't always put up a fight at first, and then when I did, it seemed like I was just trying to stop something that had been going on for a long time and was not likely to end soon—like jumping off a moving train because it was making you sick but the conductor couldn't stop for some reason.

"I feel like I'm broken—like I don't fit together anymore. Like there's no more room for me in the world or something. Like I've overstayed my welcome here on Earth, and everyone's trying to give me hints about that constantly. Like I should just check out." I try to look at Herr Silverman, but I can't take my eyes off the city lights reflected on the water. "And I think that's why my mom left for New York and why no one wants to talk to me ever. I'm so fucking worthless."

"You're not."

"But I am. Everyone hates me at school. You know that's true."

"I don't hate you. I hope my being here tonight proves that to you. And our high school is just a tiny place. Just a blip in your life, really. Good things ahead. You'll see."

I don't really believe him, and I sort of laugh, because who the hell tells a teen with a gun in his hand "good things ahead"? It's so absurd.

I look down at the P-38 and sigh. "I can't even kill myself properly."

"That's another good thing, right there," Herr Silverman says, and smiles in this fantastic way, which makes me believe him. "That's a *beautiful* thing."

Beautiful.

I wish I could believe that.

I wipe my nose with my coat sleeve.

He puts his coat back on.

"What do you think I should do with this?" I say as we both stare at the WWII Nazi relic in my hand.

"Why not just throw it in the water?"

"You don't think it belongs in the Holocaust museum?"

He laughs in this unencumbered way he never would in class.

It's like a wink.

Like maybe he's telling me that he thinks the SAT answers my classmates give are really bullshit, just like I do.

Herr Silverman says, "As far as I'm concerned, *all* guns belong at the bottom of rivers."

"I wonder if it even fires," I say.

"I'd feel a lot better if you'd at least put the gun down. I'm trying really hard to appear calm, but my heart's still racing, and it would be much easier for me if you no longer had a loaded pistol in your hand."

I think about how much Herr Silverman is risking coming out here tonight to deal with my crazy ass. There's the gun. Plus the legal red tape if I actually do kill myself, because he's involved now in a pretty serious way. If anyone found out we were having this conversation right now, I'm pretty sure my high school's lawyers would shit themselves.

"My life will get better? You really believe that?" I ask,

even though I know what he will say—what most adults would feel they *have* to say when asked such a question, even though the overwhelming amount of evidence and life experience suggests that people's lives get worse and worse until you die. Most adults just aren't happy—that's a fact.

But I know it will sound less like a lie coming from Herr Silverman.

"It can. If you're willing to do the work."

"What work?"

"Not letting the world destroy you. That's a daily battle."

I think about what he's saying and I get it on some level. I wonder what Herr Silverman would look like if I followed him home from work. I bet he'd look happy—proud of the good work he did during the day. So unlike the 1970s sunglasses woman who called me a pervert and all of the other miserable train people I've followed. I bet he'd listen to an iPod and maybe even sing along to the music. The other passengers would look at him and wonder why the hell he's so happy. They'd probably resent him. Maybe they'd even want to kill him.

"You don't think I'm capable of shooting someone, do you? You never thought I'd kill myself either," I say.

"That's why I'm here. I wouldn't have come if I didn't think you were worth it."

I look at Herr Silverman's face for a long time—not saying anything at all.

I look so long the tension between us builds and starts to feel awkward, even if Herr Silverman doesn't acknowledge it.

"Throw the gun in the river, Leonard. Trust in the future. Go ahead. Do it. It's okay. Things are going to get better. You can do the work."

Maybe because I want to rid myself of all the evidence connected to this night, maybe because I want to please Herr Silverman, maybe because it's just fucking fun to chuck stuff into rivers, I take three quick steps toward the water and throw the P-38 like a boomerang.

I see it spin through the light of the distant city and then it disappears a few seconds before we hear it plunk into the river and sink.

I think about my grandfather executing the Nazi officer who first carried that gun.

I think about how far that gun had to travel through time and space to end up at the bottom of a Delaware River tributary.

And how stories and objects and people and pretty much everything can blink out of existence at any time.

Then I think about my fictional future daughter S and me scuba diving with Horatio the dolphin after the nuclear holocaust. S has all of these cute freckles on her face. Her eyes are gray like mine. Her hair is bobbed at her chin.

"I wonder if we'll find my old P-38 gun," I say to her in my fantasy.

"Why did you have a gun when you were a kid?" she replies.

"Good question," I say, and then we both lower our masks and fall over the side of the boat into the water.

Even though I know it's just silly fiction, the thought warms my chest—I have to admit.

"So what do we do now?" I ask.

"Anyone home at your house?" Herr Silverman says.

"No. My mom's in New York."

"Then you're coming home with me."

THIRTY-THREE

In the cab, Herr Silverman does a lot of texting with someone he calls Julius.

I can tell by the look on his face and the way he's poking his cell phone that Julius is not cool with my coming over, but I don't say anything about that or ask any questions, even though Herr Silverman's facial expressions sort of make me want to jump out of the moving cab, roll to the sidewalk, run away bruised and bleeding, and take a train back to New Jersey.

I'm sort of freaked about everything I told him—like maybe it was a mistake to be honest. I'm worried he'll never look at me the same way—he's just being nice to my face, but then when I leave he'll tell Julius that I sicken him. I keep telling myself that Herr Silverman isn't like that—that he's good and understands—but it's hard to make myself believe in Herr Silverman a hundred percent now.

When we arrive at his building, the cab fare is more than

two hundred dollars, and I insist on paying with my credit card, even though Herr Silverman says I don't have to. He's a teacher, so I know that two hundred bucks is a lot for him.

My hand shakes when I extend the credit card through the little plastic window that separates the cabdriver from the passengers, but Herr Silverman doesn't say anything about how shaky I am.

I give the cabdriver an eighty-dollar tip because fuck Linda, who will be paying the bill, but my hand is still shaking and you can barely read the numbers I write.

"Is this okay?" I ask as we walk up the steps, and even my voice is all over the place wobbly.

"Is *what* okay?"

"Having a student over to your apartment."

"Is it okay with you?"

"Yeah, but aren't there school policies forbidding you to do this sort of thing? I mean...I don't want to get you in trouble."

"Well, I do believe this is an extenuating circumstance. And if you don't tell anyone, no one will know."

"Okay," I say, and stick my shaky hands in my pockets.

If any other teacher had said this to me, I'd have thought they were executing some sort of perverted plan—*but not Herr Silverman*, I tell myself. *You can trust him.*

Outside his door as he puts the key in the lock, he says, "My roommate, Julius, is inside sleeping."

I nod, because I realize that Julius is most likely Herr

Silverman's partner, and I wonder if Julius really is pissed about my taking up so much of Herr Silverman's time and now invading their personal lives. Part of me starts to wish I weren't here—that I didn't even call my Holocaust teacher.

Herr Silverman keys into his apartment and loudly says, "Julius? I'm here with Leonard."

No response.

"Come on in," Herr Silverman says, and I follow him to a leather couch over which hangs a huge painting of a bare tree, which gets me thinking about the Japanese maple outside my English class and what an asshole I was to Mrs. Giavotella, which makes me feel depressed again.

The tree in the painting is surrounded by the decapitated heads of famous political leaders: Benito Mussolini, Joseph Stalin, Gandhi, Ronald Reagan, Winston Churchill, George Washington, Adolf Hitler, Fidel Castro, Teddy Roosevelt, Nelson Mandela, Saddam Hussein, JFK, and a dozen or so more I don't recognize. It looks like the heads have fallen from the tree like rotten fruit. And a huge red *X* has been painted over the entire painting—like someone stamped it with a rejection. It's one of the strangest artworks I have ever seen.

"Have a seat," Herr Silverman says. "I'll be right back."

He opens the bedroom door a crack and slips in without letting me see what's behind—like he sort of makes a U around the door without opening it more than ten inches and then closes it quickly.

I hear whispering, and the voice that's not Herr Silverman's is sort of fierce, like wind rushing through barren tree branches.

"This isn't your job," I hear Julius say a little more loudly.

"Shhhh," Herr Silverman says. "He'll hear you."

And then they are silent for a minute before I hear the fierce whispering again.

Finally, the door opens ten inches, and Herr Silverman slips around once more before he shuts it for good.

"Your roommate is pissed that I'm here," I say.

"He's just tired. He has to work in the morning and he's afraid we'll keep him up. We'll be quiet."

"I heard him say this isn't your job, and it's not. I shouldn't have called you. I shouldn't have gotten you involved."

"It's okay," Herr Silverman says. "I'm glad you did. You can meet Julius in the morning. He'll be less grumpy with a full night's rest."

"He's your boyfriend, right?"

"Yeah."

"Okay," I say, and then feel stupid for saying okay—like Herr Silverman needs my permission or something.

"Here," Herr Silverman says, and then holds out his hand.

There's a small box in front of my face wrapped in white paper.

When I have it unwrapped and opened, it takes me a second to realize what's inside.

It's my grandfather's Bronze Star, only it's been covered

with paper, painted, and then laminated. On the star is a bronze peace sign and on the ribbon are my initials written in fancy calligraphy swirls.

"If you don't like it," Herr Silverman says, "I can remove the tape and paper. The actual medal isn't altered underneath. I was going to give it back to you tomorrow after class. Remember when you said you wanted to turn the negative connotation into a positive?"

I'm not entirely sure how to respond. It's kind of corny on one hand, and on the other it's an amazingly thoughtful present—plus it's the only gift I will receive on my eighteenth birthday, which is almost over.

But for some reason, instead of saying thank you like any polite, normal person would, and maybe because I feel like it might be really important, I say, "Does Julius make you happy? I mean—do you love him? And does he love you? Is it a good relationship?"

"Why do you ask?" Herr Silverman gets this worried look on his face, like my question throws him a little.

Instead of answering his question, I say, "Did you write letters from the future Julius when you were in high school?"

"Actually, I did," Herr Silverman says. "Metaphorically, I absolutely did."

It makes me feel less insane to think about Herr Silverman being all confused in high school about his sexuality and writing letters from the future people in his life—the people who would understand him, and listen to him, and treat him like an equal without making him act and put on a fake mask. The people who could save him. Herr Silverman believing in those people back when he was my age, and then making it to his age, because if he's truly happy...

I get mad at myself for thinking about all of that, because there's still a large part of me that thinks it's all bullshit, and if I let myself believe in the bullshit, it will just ultimately make me even more depressed when bad things happen or Herr Silverman eventually lets me down and I can't believe in him or his philosophies anymore. But for some reason, I go ahead and pin the stupid peace medal to my shirt, right over my heart. Maybe just because Herr Silverman went to so much trouble for me tonight—maybe because I owe him this much, and it doesn't really hurt to pin a fucking medal to my shirt.

"Looks good," Herr Silverman says to me, and then smiles.

"Thanks," I say, and suddenly I feel so tired—like I really don't care about anything anymore, like I'm just finished.

"I'd like to call your mother, Leonard. May I?"

"What for?"

"Well, we're going to have a lot to sort out in the morning."

"Like what?"

"You need help. Professional help. I'm not sure your mother realizes the seriousness of your condition—how much pain you've been in. These things don't just go away."

"She won't listen to you. She's crazy."

"May I call her? *Please*," Herr Silverman says.

I suck my lips into my mouth because I'm exhausted and don't really feel like arguing with him, and then I nod, thinking, *Herr Silverman can't make anything worse.*

"She's under Fashion Designer Linda," I say while I'm doing the pattern to unlock my cell. I hand him the phone and say, "But she probably won't answer anyway. She never answers at night. Says she needs her beauty sleep, but really it's because she's sleeping with this French guy who loves sex and Linda is a nymphomaniac."

I wish I hadn't said that last joke, especially because Herr Silverman doesn't even acknowledge it, let alone laugh.

He calls Linda, but she doesn't answer.

He leaves a message saying that I'm with him at his apartment and he'd really appreciate a call back, because it's an emergency. He leaves his cell phone number and then hangs up.

"Guess we wait for her to call," Herr Silverman says.

I look away.

Linda won't call back tonight.

I know from experience.

Herr Silverman pulls a pad of paper from a drawer, writes down Linda's phone number, and sticks it in his shirt pocket.

"Did you paint this?" I point back at the X-ed-out-tree-with-fallen-decapitated-heads-of-famous-political-leaders painting that hangs over the couch. I don't know why I ask. Maybe just to change the subject. Maybe because I feel bad about Linda's not calling, and Herr Silverman's belief that she will.

Herr Silverman's face lights up like he's either really proud of the painting or he's just happy to have something to talk about besides how fucked I am. "No," he says. "I purchased it when I went to Israel a few years ago. At an art show. A friend of a friend. Had it shipped home. A little extravagance."

"It's very good," I lie. I don't really like it at all. I just feel like I should be nice to Herr Silverman. I'm kind of worried that he's going to use my secret against me—everything I told him about Asher—so I want to be on his good side.

"I like it," he says.

"What does it mean?" I ask, trying to make him happy.

"Does it have to mean something?"

"I don't know. I thought art was supposed to mean something."

"Can't it just exist without an explanation? Why do we have to assign meaning to art? Do we need to understand *everything*? Maybe it exists to evoke feelings and emotions—period. Not to *mean* something."

I nod to acknowledge what he's saying, even though it sounds a little like art-talk bullshit to me.

Still—I think about Herr Silverman and Julius having deep conversations about art and life and everything, and it actually starts to make me smile.

Life beyond the übermorons.

If I weren't so tired, I'd continue the conversation, debating back and forth, just like in Herr Silverman's Holocaust class, like he always wants us to. I'd go on for hours and hours, but I feel like my mind's quitting on me—like I only have time for one or two more questions—so I ask, "Would you say it's modern art? Something you'd see in MoMA in New York City? I'm sort of interested in modern art lately."

"Well, it's *art* and it's *modern*. But anything painted recently is called *contemporary* art."

I nod and say, "Do you think a picture of a Nazi handgun set next to a bowl of oatmeal could be contemporary art, or maybe just art?"

"Sure," he says. "Why not?"

"Okay," I say, and then we just sort of sit there silently until I realize I'm dangerously exhausted—that my brain is maybe at the end of its rope—and I can't wait for Linda to not call all night, because I just don't have the energy. My eyelids weigh a million pounds each. Through a yawn, I say, "Do you mind if I shut my eyes for a second or two?"

"Go right ahead," he says. "Make yourself comfortable."

As soon as my head hits his couch, the rope snaps.

It feels like my brain is falling down into some pitch-black abyss.

I dream of übernothing.

THIRTY-FOUR

There's a warm puffy blanket over me when I wake up.

I'm sweating.

The lights are off and the curtains have been pulled, but the glow of the city creeps in from under the heavy cloth and illuminates the outside rectangle of the windows.

It takes me a second to remember where I am and how I got here on my Holocaust teacher's couch, but once I do, I feel a rush of adrenaline course through my veins.

I sit up and think, *What the hell happened yesterday?*

Then I replay it all in my mind, remembering. When I get to the part about Asher Beal, I feel like maybe I shouldn't have told Herr Silverman about what happened—like it was a horrible mistake. I trust him, but I also know he has to tell other people to get me help, and what if those other people think I'm a pervert, and do things to me that will fuck my head up even worse? How can I trust people I don't know? I don't know what's going to happen next, and that makes me feel like I'm covered in super-pissed-off scorpions and spiders. I didn't really think my confession to Herr Silverman through. It just sort of happened.

Maybe I shouldn't be here.

Maybe
I really
should
have
killed
myself.

I also start to worry that Herr Silverman went through my cell phone photos and found the one of Asher jerking off—which would really make him think I'm a pervert—so I grab my cell off the coffee table, hit the camera button, and see what was recorded.

It's just the flash reflected in the glass of Asher's bedroom window, so I delete it and feel a little relieved, but not completely.

I wish I could delete the past twenty-four hours.

I check my history and there are no calls from Linda, and I don't know how to feel about that.

Part of me is relieved, part of me is disappointed, which is confusing.

I reach into my pocket to make sure I have the massive six-figure check I tried to give Baback and I rip it up into a million tiny pieces, although I'm not quite sure why, and the pieces land all over Herr Silverman's floor and are hard to clean up because there are so many.

I'm not thinking straight.

I'm not sure I can trust myself.

I look at Herr Silverman's closed bedroom door and think about him sleeping in the same bed as Julius, how they have this life together in the city that has nothing to do with me or my shitty high school or Herr Silverman's teaching—and how I invaded their world last night, crossed all sorts of lines. I can understand why Julius was so pissed at me, because I was acting like a psychopath, and it sort of makes me feel horrible, because Herr Silverman was only trying to do the right thing, which is amazing, because no one ever does the right thing, but I should be with Linda and my dad right now. And because they blow as parents, I'm fucked up and Herr Silverman has to deal with my shit, which isn't fair to him and maybe will lead to bad things for me in the end. It's weird, because I really love Herr Silverman, and the fact that he cares so much about fucked-up kids—enough to meet me under a bridge in the middle of a school night. But I shouldn't be here. This was all a mistake. My fault. I know that. And he probably shouldn't have come to rescue me either. He's too nice for his own good maybe. And I hope I don't get him into trouble.

I wonder if he talked to Linda after I passed out and what the hell he said to her.

If he was able to make her feel even the slightest bit of guilt for being so oblivious—if he could get through all that makeup and high fashion.

How much he told her about what happened.

If she even gave a shit.

I'm pretty sure that Herr Silverman is going to get my high school involved now and the school psychologist will evaluate me to figure out whether I'm truly a risk to myself or others and then when they discover how unbalanced I am, they'll pump me full of drugs and lock me away, and I start to worry about where that will be and what it will be like. What if it's worse than my current life?

What
if Herr
Silver
man is
wrong
about
my
future?

All of a sudden—I have to take off before he wakes up.

Leaving immediately—just getting far away from Herr Silverman and the talk we had last night—is the most important thing in the world.

I'm imposing.

I shouldn't be here.

Maybe I shouldn't even be alive.

Maybe I just want to enjoy my last few hours of freedom before they lock me up in some psych ward.

Maybe I just need some space.

Regardless, I stand slowly and tiptoe into the kitchen, past the closed bedroom door, and then find a pad of paper stuck to the refrigerator.

I write:

Herr Silverman,
Don't worry; I'm okay. Needed to be by myself.
Going home. Danger has passed.
Nothing to worry about. NOTHING.
I'm sorry.
Thank you.
LP
P.S. Sorry also to Julius. I won't do this again.
Promise.

I tiptoe through the living room and I'm relieved when the front door doesn't squeak or squeal.

I'm gone.

THIRTY-FIVE

I take the stairs down to the ground floor and then I'm on the predawn streets of Philadelphia.

No one is around, and I imagine this whole city is under ocean water—I imagine I'm scuba diving, and it's not really all that hard to do because it's dark and desolate and my skin is kind of wet from sleeping under the down comforter Herr Silverman threw over me and also from freaking out, which maybe I'm still doing, although I'm trying not to think about yesterday—how choosing life might have been a mistake.

Underground, I crawl below the subway turnstile—feeling the disgusting city grime on the palms of my hands—because I have no money on me, and I wait in the trash-ridden piss-smelling underbelly of Philadelphia, imagining myself scuba diving with a huge light, swimming through subway tunnels with Horatio and maybe even showing S the graffiti when she is old enough to scuba dive in such dangerous enclosed waters.

The train comes after what feels like hours of waiting, and I'm the only passenger on the car.

When we burst out from under Philly and up onto the Ben Franklin Bridge the sun is just coming up over the eastern horizon and I blink at it.

When my town is called, I stand and hold on as the train slows to a stop.

It's too early for the zombie-faced suits, although I know they'll flock here soon enough.

There's a rent-a-cop at the turnstiles and so I have to make a decision because I don't have the ticket I need to get through the machines.

I'm just about to make a run for it when I see an old ticket on the ground.

I pick it up and insert it into the machine.

It doesn't work, of course.

"Officer," I say, and hold up the rectangle of paper. "My ticket's not working."

"Just go under," he says, and then takes a slurp from his bucket-sized Styrofoam coffee cup and turns his back.

I crawl under the turnstile and walk out into the early-morning sunshine.

I'm not really sure what my plan is, but somehow I wind up walking past Lauren's house, which is right next door to her father's church.

Standing across the street looking at the house, I sort of feel like the house is looking back at me—like the two second-floor windows are eyes and the row of downstairs windows is a mouth. Kind of like what you see in old horror movies—the house coming to life like a face.

I have this stupid fantasy where I ring the doorbell and Lauren answers in a white bathrobe—which gives me a nice V-shot of her chest—and wearing the silver cross I gave her. We talk and I thank her for praying for me and she says it's great that I'm still alive and we both agree that kissing was a mistake, before we shake hands and wish each other well—like everything is forgiven. But it's all just bullshit and I know I messed up with Lauren in a way that can't be fixed easily, which is so unbearably depressing.

"Fuck," I say in real life, standing on the sidewalk across the street from Lauren's house, shaking my head.

I know I'm an asshole for forcing Lauren to kiss me—a hypocrite even.

A bad person.

I walk away.

I'll probably never talk to Lauren again and I'm okay with that.

It's best.

Maybe I only pursued her because I knew a relationship between us was impossible. Like she was a safe test for me, because she had so much religion crammed into her brain that things would never go too far. But I ended up failing the test, so what does that mean?

I don't know.

It's kind of horrible that she's the first girl I ever kissed, because I'll always remember her as my first girl kiss, which will remind me of everything else that happened afterward. And I start to worry that every single time I kiss a girl from now on will trigger a flood of memories that will take me back to last night. Like maybe I'll never be able to enjoy kissing at all.

All that gets me feeling depressed again, so I head over to Walt's and key in.

THIRTY-SIX

I hear the TV blaring.

Walt sometimes has trouble hearing, so I'm not surprised by the volume.

What surprises me is this: He's watching Bogart films this early in the morning.

I hear Katharine Hepburn's uppity voice and know he's watching *The African Queen* again.

"HELLO?" I say as loud as possible as I walk under the chandelier.

Walt doesn't answer, and when he sees me standing in the room's entranceway, he sort of jumps in his recliner, looks at me for a few seconds, turns off the movie with the remote, and says, "*Leonard?*"

"It's me. In the flesh."

"I couldn't sleep. Been watching Bogie all night. *I was really worried about you.* I thought that—I called your home, but no one answered and—"

We just look at each other for a long time because he doesn't want to say what he's thinking and I don't want to talk about last night.

Finally, he regains his composure, falls back into the safety of our routine, picks up his Bogart hat off the arm of his recliner, pops it onto his head, and pulls his old-time movie-star face.[69]

"Is something the matter, Mr. Allnut? Tell me," he says, his jaw barely moving, his voice higher than natural, playing Rose Sayer, Katharine Hepburn's character in *The African Queen*.

I adjust my Bogart hat—even though Bogie doesn't wear this type of hat in this movie—and say, "Nothing. *Nothing you'd understand*."

"I simply can't imagine what could be the matter. It's been such a pleasant day. What is it?" he says, staying in character.

But suddenly, I don't really want to trade Bogart movie quotes anymore, so I take off my hat and, using my regular speaking voice, I say, "Yesterday was bad, Walt. Really terrible."

His eyes open so wide. *"What the hell happened to your hair?"*

Words escape me—I mean, how would I even begin to explain it all to the old man?

---

69 It's funny because we never used Bogart hats before yesterday, but somehow I understand that his putting the hat on is symbolic—a sign that we are about to talk in code. Walt and I have something going on that's hard to explain. We understand each other. We just do. And I love that so much. Good-guy pheromones.

In an effort to avoid eye contact, I stare at the picture of Walt's dead wife, who hangs eternally young on the wall.

Sea-foam green blouse.

Blond Bogart-era hairstyle.

Mysterious eyes that pop and seem to be watching me.

She doesn't look much older than eighteen in the photo but she's dead now. I know Walt misses her terribly because I catch him gazing at the picture with this sad look in his eyes. I wonder what my future wife will look like and if I'll hang her picture on my wall—maybe in Lighthouse 1.

"And what's with the goofy medal on your shirt?"

Walt's staring at my heart now. His eyebrows are zigzags.

I look down and remember Herr Silverman's creation. I'm not sure I can explain the significance of the medal without getting into all the bullshit I went through last night, so I say, "I know I acted strange yesterday. I'm sorry. And I'll tell you everything you want to know later, Walt. I swear to god. I'll answer every question you got. But for now, could we just watch the rest of the movie together wearing our Bogart hats? Can we do that? It would mean a lot to me if you just let me watch the movie with you. I'm really tired. I don't have much left in the proverbial tank. It was a hell of a night. It really was. I need some Bogart. Bogie medicine. Whadda ya say?"

He looks at me for a second or two—examines my face, trying to figure my angle out—and then says, "Sure. Sure. Bogart. We can do that," real cautiously, like maybe he thinks

I'm trying to trick him, even though I'm being utterly sincere and honest—maybe for the first time in years.

I put my Bogart hat back on and sit down at the end of the couch closest to his recliner.

He hits play on his remote and the picture on the TV comes to life.

It's the part where their boat gets stuck in mud, and when Bogart tries to free it by getting into the water, he returns covered in leeches. Since they're stuck in the middle of nowhere, they think they're going to die. But Rose prays and it starts to rain and the river rises and they're miraculously saved. A whole bunch of other stuff happens with evil Germans, which I already know. My eyes glaze over and I zone out, mostly thinking about how close I came to killing Asher and myself last night. How it almost seemed like I was watching a movie when I had the gun pointed at my classmate—like it wasn't even real. How fucked-up scary that seems now that my head is straight. As I sit here next to Walt, I feel kind of grateful for this moment, as strange as that sounds—like I just narrowly avoided some awful, demented fate.

I feel kind of lucky.

It worries me that I can be so explosive one day—volatile enough to commit a murder-suicide—and then the next day I'm watching Bogart save the day with Walt, like nothing happened at all, and nothing is urgent, and I really don't have to do anything to set the world right or escape my own mind.

I'd like to feel okay all the time—to have the ability to sit and function without feeling so much pressure, without feeling as though blood is going to spurt from my eyes and fingers and toes if I don't do something.

When the movie ends, Walt clicks off the TV and says, "You know, I was thinking."

"And?" I say.

"Why did you give me this hat yesterday? I mean, what was so special about yesterday?"

"It was my birthday. I turned eighteen."

"Jesus Christ! Why didn't you tell anybody? I feel like a cheapskate now. I would've bought you a present."

I smile and say, "I bought your hat at the thrift store for four dollars and fifty cents. It's not really an old movie prop. Bogie never wore it."

"Yeah, I know, Rockefeller," he says. "I like it anyway. So what did you do to celebrate your birthday?"

I almost laugh, because Walt asked the question so innocently, like I'm just a regular kid who had a regular birthday.

Walt's the only person in the world who would think I'm capable of being regular like that, and I kind of love him for it.

"Can I tell you what happened to me on my birthday later? I'm still kind of tired. And I don't feel like talking about it right now."

Walt looks at me a second, takes off his Bogart hat, and then says, "Lauren Bacall approaching Bogart at the bar in *The Big Sleep*," and then in a girlish, husky Bacall voice he says, "I'm late. I'm sorry."

I remember the scene and the lines, so playing Bogart I say, "How are you today?"

"Better than last night."

"Well, I can agree on that," I say.

"That's a start," he says, breaking character. "That's a start."

I force a smile, but it's awkward and Walt knows it.

Am I better than last night?

I dunno.

But I don't feel angry anymore.

"You going to school today?" Walt says, just before the silence gets strange.

"I'm thinking I'll take the day off. And I have to go home now. I haven't been home since yesterday. I need a shower," I say, even though I don't really give a shit about taking a shower. *"Movie later tonight?"*

He flips open his Zippo with his thumb—making that scrappy clink noise—lights up a cigarette, takes a pull, and exhales his smoky words. "Sounds like the start of a beautiful friendship, Leonard. It really does."

"Here's looking at you, kid."

He smiles in this really good, honest way—better than Bogie even.

I take it in and, when our smiling at each other starts to feel too awkward, I turn and walk away.

"Leonard?"

I spin around to face Walt.

"I'm glad you visited me this morning."

As he blows another lungful of smoke at the ceiling, his eyes twinkle under his Bogart hat brighter than the orange cherry on his Pall Mall, and I get the sense that even though we just watch old Bogart movies together and never really talk about anything but Bogie-related topics, maybe Walt knows me better than anyone else in the world, as strange as that sounds. Maybe we've been communicating effectively through Bogart-related quotes all along. Maybe I'm better than I thought when it comes to communication, at least with people like Walt.

And maybe there are other people like Walt out there—waiting for me to find them.

Maybe.

THIRTY-SEVEN

The kitchen mirror in my house is still in pieces, so when I look into the sink a million little jagged minnows return my stare.

I open the fridge and see my hair wrapped in pink paper, and I think, *What the fuck?* and *Who was I yesterday?* and *What the fuck?* again.

I should clean it all up, but I simply don't have the strength.

It's so much easier to shut the refrigerator door, which is totally a metaphor, I realize, for my life.

Maybe I want Linda to find the wrapped-up hair and see it all—how horrible I was yesterday.

What a shitty birthday I had.

That she forgot she gave birth to me eighteen years ago.

That she is the worst mother in the world.

How much help I need.

But Linda probably wouldn't make the connection even if

she found my hair wrapped in pink paper. She'd probably think I cut my hair as a present *for her*.

I make my way upstairs to my bedroom.

When I empty my pockets I realize that my cell phone ran out of power some point after I left Herr Silverman's apartment, so I plug it in.

After it loads up, the you-have-messages signal buzzes.

There's a voice mail from Linda, who says, "What did you tell your teacher about me? What's going on? What is it this time? I'm in the back of a car on my way home instead of attending the several extremely important meetings I had planned. What the hell is going—"

I delete before she can finish.

Then there's a message from Herr Silverman and his voice sounds different, sort of pissed. "Leonard? Why did you leave? Where did you go? I'm worried about you. I took a risk last night and I have to say I'm disappointed in you. You shouldn't have left. You've put me in an awkward position, because I promised your mother that—"

For some reason I delete him too.

Then I feel guilty and call him back, even though he's probably in school by now, because it's later than I thought.

The phone rings and rings and finally I get his voice mail.

"It's me. Leonard Peacock. Thanks for coming to the bridge last night. That was really cool... necessary, even. I'm sorry I got you in trouble with your partner. I'm sorry I've been such an asshole. I'm going to do the work. Don't worry about me. I just had a bad night. I'll be okay. But I'm taking a day off. I just had to leave this morning. Just got the urge to move. Had to greet the day, if you know what I mean. I hope your partner didn't think I was rude. I won't tell anyone that you're gay. I don't care that you're gay. It doesn't matter to me. That was probably a stupid thing to say, right? Because why *should* I care? I'd never say I don't care that you're black to a person of color. I'm an asshole. Sorry. Just forget about that part. See you Monday. Thanks again. *And don't worry about me!* There's nothing to worry about anymore. Nothing." Then I just sort of hold the phone to my ear without hanging up. I listen to silence for a minute, thinking that all of what I said was just plain idiotic, and then there is a beep and this robot woman comes on and asks if I'm satisfied with my message. I don't have the strength to answer that honestly, let alone record another, so I just hang up.

It's so quiet in my room that I wonder if this is what being dead sounds like.

I hear Linda key into the front door and then she's yelling, "Leo? Leo, are you here? Why didn't you call me back?"

I hate her.

I hate her so much.

She's so stupid it's almost comical.

She's such a caricature.

Such a nonperson.

What type of mother forgets her son's eighteenth birthday?

What type of mother ignores so many warning signs?

It's almost impossible to believe she exists.

I hear her high heels click across the hardwood floor and then I hear silence as she stops by the hallway mirror to check her makeup. No matter what Herr Silverman told her, no matter how much he sugarcoated it, whatever he said was enough to get her to drive all the way here from New York City. So you'd think she'd run up the stairs to make sure I'm okay, right? Like any rational, caring mother would. Like any HUMAN would. But you'd be wrong.

Linda can't pass a mirror without pausing because she's addicted to mirrors, so don't judge her too harshly. She has issues. It doesn't even piss me off, because that's just Linda. I could be on fire, screaming my head off, and she'd still have to pause in front of the mirror to check her makeup before she could extinguish me. That's my mom.

More clicking of high heels and then she's walking up the steps, which has a runner of carpet so no clicking.

"Leo?" she says joyfully, like she's singing, and I wonder if she's singing because she's hoping I'm not here—like maybe she hopes I offed myself and she'll never have to deal with me again. "Leo, where are you?"

More clicking as she walks down the hallway, then silence as she crosses the Oriental runner that leads to my bedroom.

"Leo?" she says, and then knocks.

I stare at the door so hard, thinking of how justified I'd be if I just went off on her, listing all the ways that she's failed me, but I can't bring myself to say anything.

"Leo?" Linda says. "I hope you are decent. I'm coming in."

She pushes the door open and there she is in my bedroom doorframe. She's wearing a white jacket with some sort of fur collar—it looks like mink. Her hair is perfect as always. She's got on a knee-length bright green wool skirt—classy and age-appropriate—and white heels. She looks amazing, as always. And it makes me laugh because her appearance suggests she'd have the perfect son—like she lives a perfect life and therefore has all the time in the world to make herself into a masterpiece of high fashion every day. People see Linda and they admire her. It's true. You would too, if you saw her. And that's her power.

"I'm happy you finally cut your hair, but who cut it? They did a terrible job, Leo," she says, and I want to strangle her. "What's going on with you? What's this all about? I'm here. I'm home. Now what seems to be the problem?"

I shake my head, because even I'm amazed.

What the hell am I supposed to say to that?

"I spoke with your teacher, Mr. Silverman. He was a bit dramatic. He said you had your grandfather's old war gun. As if that paperweight would ever fire, I told him. Well, you fooled him with your prank, because he was really concerned, Leo. Enough to insist I come home from New York immediately. You've caused quite a stir. I'm here. So let me have it—what's so important? I'm listening."

I pretend that my eyes are P-38s and my sight is bullets

and I blast holes through Linda's outfit and watch the blood soak through.

She's so oblivious.

So clueless.

So awful.

"Why are you staring at me like that, Leo?" She's got her hands on her hips now. "Seriously, you look like the world's about to end. What do you want from me? I came home. Your teacher says you want to talk. So let's talk. Were you really pretending to shoot people with that rusty old Nazi gun your father used to carry around in his guitar case? What's this about? What's going on? You're a pacifist, Leo. You wouldn't hurt a fly. *Take one look at the kid and you realize he's incapable of violence.* I told your teacher that, but he seemed really concerned. He says you need therapy. *Therapy?* I said. Like that ever did anyone any good. Your father and I tried therapy once and look how that ended up. I've never met a man or woman who escaped therapy better off than when they started."

I keep staring.

"Your teacher said you might be suicidal, but I told him that was ridiculous. You're not suicidal, are you, Leo? Just tell me if you are. We have money. We can get you medicine. Whatever you need. You can have whatever you want. Just ask for it. But I know you're not suicidal. I know what the *real* problem is."

I fucking hate her.

"I told him you do this when you miss your mother, so I came home, Leo. I always come home when you pull one of these pranks. And it wasn't easy this time either. I had to cancel twelve meetings with important people. *Twelve!* Not that you would care about that. But someday you are going to have to learn how to live without your mother and—"

"Do you remember when I was little—you used to make me banana pancakes with chocolate chips in them?" I say, because suddenly I have this idea.

Linda just looks at me like my head has spun around 360 degrees.

"You remember, right?" I say.

"What are you talking about, Leo? *Pancakes?* I wasn't driven two hours to talk about pancakes."

"You remember, Mom. We made them together once."

Linda's lipstick smiles when she hears me say the word *Mom* because she hasn't heard me say that word in many years.

Ironically, she *loves* to be called Mom.

"Banana–chocolate chip pancakes?" Linda says, and then laughs.

I can tell by the look on her face that she doesn't remember, but she's faking like she does. Maybe she only made them once or twice—I dunno. Maybe I made up the memory in my mind. It's possible. I don't know why I'm thinking about this memory all of a sudden, but I am.

I remember making banana–chocolate chip pancakes

when I was little—like maybe when I was four or five years old—and getting mix everywhere and Dad was softly strumming his acoustic guitar at the kitchen table and my parents were happy that morning, which was rare, and probably why I remember it. Mom and I cooked and then we all ate together as a family.

Normal for most people, but extraordinary for us.

For some reason, I must have banana–chocolate chip pancakes in order for everything to be okay. Right now. It's the only thing that will help. I don't know why. That's just the way it is. I tell myself that if Linda makes me banana–chocolate chip pancakes, I can forgive her for forgetting my birthday. I concoct that deal in my head and then attempt to make her fulfill her end of the unspoken bargain.

"Can you make those for me now—banana–chocolate chip pancakes?" I ask. "That's all I want from you. Make them, eat breakfast with me, and then you can go back to New York. Okay? Deal?"

"Do we have the ingredients?" she says, looking completely perplexed.

"Shit," I say, because we don't. I haven't been shopping in weeks. "Shit, shit, shit."

"Do you have to say *shit* in front of your mother?"

"If I get the ingredients, will you make me breakfast?"

"That's why you wanted me to come home? *Banana–chocolate chip pancakes?* That's why you tricked your teacher into getting so worked up?"

"You make them for me and I won't give you any more problems all day. You can go back to New York with a clean conscience. Problem solved."

Linda laughs in a way that lets me know she's relieved, and then she runs her perfectly manicured nails through my newly stubbled hair, which tickles.

"You really are an odd boy, Leo."

"Is that a yes?"

"I still don't understand what happened yesterday. Why did your teacher call me and demand I come home? You seem fine to me."

Herr Silverman must not have told her it was my birthday, and I don't even care about that anymore. I just want the fucking pancakes. It's something Linda is capable of doing. It's a task she can complete for me. It's what I can have, so that's what I want.

"I'll go get the ingredients, okay?" I say, making it even easier for her.

"Okay," she says, and then shrugs playfully, like she's my girlfriend instead of my mom.

I rush past her, down the steps, and out the door without even putting on a coat.

There's a local grocery about six blocks from our house and I find everything I need there in about ten minutes.

Milk.

Eggs.

Butter.

Pancake mix.

Maple syrup.

Chocolate chips.

Bananas.

On the walk home, with the plastic handles of the grocery bag cutting into my hand, I think about how once again, I'm letting Linda off easy.

I try to concentrate on the pancakes.

I can taste the chocolate and bananas melting in my mouth.

Pancakes are good.

They will fill me.

They are what I can have.

When I arrive home, Linda's in her office yelling at someone on the phone about the color of tulle. "No, I do not want cadmium fucking orange!" She holds up her index finger when she sees me in the doorway and then waves me away.

In the kitchen I wait five minutes before I decide to do the prep work by myself.

I slice three bananas on the cutting board. Carefully, I make paper-thin cuts. And then I stir milk and eggs into the mix—adding the chocolate chips and banana slices last. I spray the pan and heat it up.

"Linda?" I yell. *"Mom?"*

She doesn't answer, so I decide to cook the pancakes, thinking that Linda eating with me can be enough.

I pour some batter onto the pan and it bubbles and sizzles

while I pour out three more pancakes. I flip all four and then heat up the oven so I can keep the finished pancakes warm while I cook Mom's.

"Linda?"

No answer.

"Mom?"

No answer.

I put the finished pancakes into the oven and pour more batter.

I realize I made way too much, but I just keep cooking pancakes, and by the time I finish, I have enough to feed a family of ten.

"Mom?"

I go to her study, and she's yelling again.

"Jasmine can go fuck herself!" she says, and then sighs.

She's staring out the window.

She's oblivious again.

I sigh.

I return to the kitchen.

I eat my banana–chocolate chip pancakes.

They are delicious.

Fuck Linda.

She's missing out.

She could have had delicious pancakes for breakfast.

I would have forgiven her.

But instead, I use the garbage disposal to grind up all the leftover pancakes.

A few mirror shards fall in.

I let the machine crunch away until it finally jams and I can once again hear Linda cursing at her employees.

She doesn't come out of her office—not even when I take off and slam the front door behind me so that the whole house shakes.

THIRTY-EIGHT
LETTER FROM THE FUTURE NUMBER 4

Dad,

It's S, your daughter.

I'm writing you on my eighteenth birthday—well, technically, it's the day after; it's past midnight. I'm manning the great light because you fell asleep in your chair again and old habits die hard. I'm going to give you this letter tomorrow when I leave Outpost 37 for the first time so you won't ever forget what a great day we had together.

(Side note: The stars are amazing tonight—like we could swim in them. Cassiopeia is shining brightly.)

I have this suspicion: I think you're mad at me because I want to leave, although you've never said as much. You think I'm leaving just so I can find a boy-friend, or at least that's what you tease me about. (And I swear—if you use the word *hormones* one more time, I might kill you!) And while I *would* like to have a boyfriend (BECAUSE THAT IS NORMAL!) and meet people my own age in the horrid "tube city," there are many other things I'd like to do as well.

I'd like to see dry land.

I've never seen it.

I want to stand on earth.

That's a simple but profound thought for a girl who has lived her whole life on water.

You can surely understand that on some level, even if dry land is "overrated."

I'm looking forward to attending classes with other people my age, even though you've told me so many times that people aren't always kind or considerate like Papa was and you and Mom are. Still, I'd like to see for myself—have conversations with so many different people! I'd like to find someone who kisses me every time he sees a shooting star, like you kiss Mom. And I think that maybe I can excel in post-school, especially since I did so well on the entrance exams, and afterward I can make you proud by putting good into the new world somehow.

Thank you for making me "pancakes" on my birthday.

Even though you had to use bread mix and you said it wasn't as good as pancakes back when you were a kid, especially since we had no "syrup" because there are so few "maple trees" left. I appreciated the effort, especially after hearing the story of how your mom and you made them when you were little—with "chocolate chips" and yellow fruits called "bananas." I hope to see and taste a banana one day. I choose to believe that they still exist in tube city, where all sorts of things exist—things that I have only dreamed about, like stores and restaurants and dogs and cats and movie theaters and sky walks and so many other nouns we've seen on the visualizer beam whenever the signal is strong enough.

And your birthday present to me was also... *beautiful.*

When you said we were going to use the last two oxygen tanks, I didn't want to do it, because it meant that you'd never be able to go scuba diving again, unless the North American Land Collective sends you more bottles, which isn't likely to happen, now that they've declared world order and Outpost 37, Lighthouse 1 is no longer technically operational.

But I'm glad that I went scuba diving with you down into "Philadelphia" one last time with old Horatio the dolphin following.

I didn't believe you when you said there was a red statue that read "LOVE," with the LO stacked on top of the VE.

LO
VE

It sounded like something out of one of the old fairy tales you used to tell me when I was a little girl. I thought you were kidding when you said people in the past believed in love so much that they made statues to celebrate it, so they wouldn't forget to LOVE…well, that seemed kind of ridiculous—but when we dove down and you shined the thermal lantern, and it turned out to be true, I felt like there were so many possibilities in the world—like I'm only beginning to discover what's achievable. Maybe I will find a pure love—like what you and Mom have.

Mom told me that you and Horatio searched for the statue for weeks and then cleaned all the seaweed off, using up most of your oxygen supply, and so I wanted to say it was the best birthday present I have ever received. How many fathers would go to so much work just for their daughter's eighteenth birthday?

Not many.

You told me you spent the day after your eighteenth birthday sitting on a bench in LOVE Park in Philadelphia writing in your notebook.

From what you've told me of your past and dry land—and what I've pieced together too—I realize that your childhood was pretty terrible.

That you had to endure a lot to get to Outpost 37 and become my father.

I want to say thank you.

You are a good man, Dad.

I've had a beautiful childhood.

And I admire you—I hope to be just like you.

I've spent my whole life watching you man the great beam—here at Lighthouse 1.

No one ever comes.

We never see any boats.

But you man the light anyway—just in case.

And *we* got to see it—all these years.

The great light.

The beautiful sweeping beam!

We were here to see it, and that was enough.

I never really understood how important that was *and is* until now.

It's hard for me to leave you here, even though I realize you and Mom will be okay.

I hope you will come visit me once I am settled in, but I understand if you can't, and I will come back to visit you as much as I can.

I've cut a thin braid of my hair off for you.

(Mom said that you cut all your hair off on your eighteenth birthday, but I wasn't about to do that, because my hair is my best feature!)

Since you're reading this, you already have the braid that was folded up inside.

You once told me that women used to send locks of their hair to the men they loved when knights rode horses across endless dry land and kings and queens ruled the people. You told me about knights back when you were telling me fairy tales, before we started reading *Hamlet* together.

I love you, Daddy.

Never forget it.

Also, I'll be okay.

Mom says you never thought you'd find her when you were my age, but you did.

You probably never thought you'd find me either, and now I need to find the people in my future too—because that's just the way of the world maybe.

You'll be okay.

What was it that you and your neighbor used to say? The old man? Was his name Walt?

"We'll always have Paris."

Well, we'll always have the LOVE statue at the bottom of Global Common Area Two.

We'll always have Outpost 37 and Lighthouse 1 and Horatio the dolphin and Philadelphia Phyllis and Who lived here? and all the rest.

I'm watching you breathe as you sleep in the chair next to me.

You look so peaceful.

You look just like a good dad should.

I can tell by the little smile on your face that you are having a wonderful dream.

I've watched you sleep for over an hour, just because.

And the whole time I wished your mind was a sea we could scuba dive in together because I'd like to see the LOVE statue that sits at the bottom of your consciousness.

I know it's huge and red and beautiful, because you've been pulling the seaweed off it for so many years. I know you weeded the waters of your mind for me, for Mom, so we could celebrate my eighteenth birthday together—and so I could go on and enjoy the life you gave me.

Keep weeding, Dad.

Weed your mind.

And man the great light.

Even when no one is looking.

Love, your daughter,

S

273

ACKNOWLEDGMENTS

The following professionals read drafts of this novel and provided valuable insights: Alicia Bessette (novelist); Liz Jensen (novelist); Doug Stewart (agent); Alvina Ling (editor); Bethany Strout (editor's assistant); Barbara Bakowski (senior production editor); Dr. Len Altamura (doctor of social work, licensed clinical social worker); Jill A. Boccia (licensed clinical social worker); Valerie Peña (licensed clinical social worker); Dr. Narsimha R. Pinninti (chief medical officer, Twin Oaks, and professor of psychiatry, UMDNJ-SOM); Meryl E. Udell, PsyD (clinical psychologist); Debra Nolan-Stevenson (licensed professional counselor); and Geetha Kumar, MD (associate professor of psychiatry, vice chair, Department of Psychiatry, UMDNJ-SOM; child/adolescent psychiatrist).

The core idea for this book was greatly nurtured by the many coffee talks I had with Evan Roskos. To my inner circle—and you know who you are—thanks for saving me a million times.